Near A Canal

Wheldon
Curzon-Hobson

To Julie

With best
wishes Gloria
Cellow Bld Ifer.

Wheldon

27/11/06

Near A Canal

Copyright © Wheldon Curzon-Hobson, 2006

The moral right of the author has been asserted

ISBN 1-877391-51-4

Ebury Street

First printed 2006

All rights reserved. No part of this book may be reproduced,
stored in a retrieval system or transmitted in any form by
any means electronic, mechanical, photocopying,
recording or otherwise, without prior permission
from the copyrite owner.

Printed by

P Printlink
REMARKABLE EVERY DAY

www.printlink.co.nz

Chapter One

June 2000, a very hot day in London. I decided to take a break from work and wander up to Regents Park where I lay down under the shade of a tree.

I took off my shoes and socks and glanced around. There were a few regulars, lots of tourists, some people crazily jogging in the heat. Others lay spread-eagled, naked but for their underwear.

I opened my book. *Hunger*, by Knut Hamsun. On the front cover it said it had won the Nobel Prize for literature, first published in 1890. It was all about a guy starving to death which was somewhat hypnotising as he got hungrier and hungrier.

A girl cycled towards me on an old fashioned bike. She had long dark hair, possibly Spanish, and wore her clothes like she enjoyed them, no fuss, just threw them on. She slowed as she got nearer and smiled, strange how clearly I can remember it. There are some smiles that stay with you, that you dwell on and make you feel good about the world. Then she stopped and held out her hand.

'This is for you.'

In her hand was a four leafed clover. I let it fall into my open palm, then she pushed down on her pedal and was off.

I studied the clover for a moment, put it between the pages of my book and clambered to my feet. I had a tingling down my spine. A beautiful girl doesn't give you a four leafed clover every day.

I sat in my Camden flat that night reading my hypnotic book about hunger. It got me thinking about going on a fast. They say it brings clarity of thought. It seemed like a good idea. My life, although immensely enjoyable, didn't seem to have a sense of direction.

I mulled it over for some time, considering how long I could last given my enormous appetite for good food and wine. A day, two days? 48 hours, that was a long time, but one day seemed a bit pathetic. Two days then. But from when? Now? I remembered how much food there was in the fridge and recognised there was no way I could survive staying at home. I'd have to go somewhere else, find a moor, but no, that wasn't the point. What exactly was the point? The point was that my life was filled with too much indulgence, of food, drink, and wandering thoughts. I needed clarity. So I decided to go without food where I normally lived, where I normally worked, and see what happened.

Not before I had finished my dinner, which was delicious, and had my last bar of chocolate and a couple of glasses of wine.

So I ate, I drank, and then I was ready.

'Bring on the hunger!'

Nothing happened that night, of course. I went to bed and slept normally, then I woke and remembered there was to be no breakfast. Not too much of a challenge. I had a longer shower and lazed around until I left for work. Walking up the street, my shoes clicking on the cobblestones, I felt great! The clear blue sky had returned, the planes were coming over every few minutes, people were smiling. I was in a good mood.

I reached my office, a publishing firm, MandrellPress, specialising in the history of art. We were pretty loose about the definition. We would publish 'art history' books, but also all sorts of titles to do with artists and their scandalous lives. Forget *The Sun* and its celebrities, our artists lived lives of fantastic debauchery, anything you could imagine, or probably had never paused to imagine. A result of their art, or their art a result of their lives – good old chicken and the egg, who knows, it made for fun reading and our readers lapped it up, all in the name of academic research.

I went up to my office on the third floor of the residential house we had converted. There were lounge chairs everywhere, it gave us a chance to lie down and have a snooze. We had snoring competitions. We had designed a miniature paper dart that we placed on a piece of Perspex in front of the snorer's nose and we measured how far it flew across the Perspex. The record was 28 centimetres, believe it or not, one of those wheezing, snoring moments compliments of Maggie, could she ever snore! She was our media nut, responsible for putting our books into the public arena. She was good at it, she knew exactly who wanted what and who needed a lunch on the firm's credit card. If there's one thing we weren't, it was stingy. We took everyone out for lunch, pre-dinner drinks, dinner, post-dinner drinks, we didn't care, that was what life was about, having fun, spending our time with genuinely interesting people.

We published books if we thought they were brilliant and no one else did. There was a market for everything, it was a matter of finding it. We sat around the board room, agreed on the books we loved, and separated them into those that would sell in established markets and those we loved but had to find a market. Selling via the internet was a bonus with these books, get them into enough keen hands and they sold like wildfire. The bookshops had to stock them as so many punters were crazy for them. I spent a lot of my time visiting universities and clubs and societies. The authors loved us for it and they would go the extra mile to promote their work because we were so enthusiastic.

Books were everywhere throughout the office. The whole place was chaotic, there was no getting away from it. I had lots of friends in more reputable publishing houses and their offices were so tidy, but try as we might we couldn't keep things in neat bookshelves. If we saw a new book we had to read it there and then. Then we'd leave it on a couch where someone else would see it and have a read.

My office, I'm proud to say, was as bad as everyone else's. There was the latest book that had come our way, *Warrior Artist* - yep, you've got to cringe, some authors are brilliant but the titles they give their work is awful. I searched through the drawers of my desk to find my pen and scrawled over the title, writing instead, *Awful Title, Great Book*. Brilliant really, about an 18 year old girl who drew pictures as the bombs landed around her during the Blitz, killing her parents and friends. She had sketched what was happening and wrote notes beside the pictures. Not many laughs but lots of quirky little tidbits - reminds you life goes on in the midst of war, what people got up to, a diary from the depths of the Blitz. I couldn't wait to get it on the shelves. The artist had died a few years ago but her daughter was keen to work on publicity. It was going to be a hit.

Tim ducked his head round the door.

'Fancy a coffee?'

'Just arrived.'

'Got anything urgent?'

'Nup.'

'Great. Let's go.'

Tim, eccentric as they come, and a compulsive reader. He loved his job, loved the people, they loved him. Everyone loved Tim.

The café was half empty, or half full, one of those silly games we play. It looked like a few hadn't slept the night before. We ordered coffee.

'Fancy anything to eat?'

'No thanks, I'm on a fast.'

'Okay.'

I paused. That wasn't enough, just a regular '*okay*.' This was my big, and I mean big endeavour – of significance!

''I'm on a fast,' I said again.

'So no marshmallows then? I've finally managed to convince them to give me marshmallows with my coffee. I always thought it unfair you only get marshmallows with hot chocolate.'

'No, not eating at all.'

'Admirable.'

Tim took the coffees and chose a seat near the door.

'Have you ever been on a fast?' I asked.

'No, never. Now, I need your advice.'

'All ears.'

'A woman …'

Tim paused, well, not exactly paused, as sort of lost consciousness, his eyes stopped focussing. If you didn't know Tim you'd think there was something wrong, be inclined to ring an ambulance or check his pulse. But no, he was merely lingering on a thought.

'A woman is troubling me.'

I waited, catching a glimpse of a gorgeous girl walking outside.

'Too young, too beautiful, and I have a problem!'

'Of course you do Tim, back to you.'

'There comes a time when you meet a woman who intrigues you. I have met one and am unsure what to do, how to proceed, or whether to proceed at all.'

'Do you need to proceed?'

'Hmm, maybe, no, yes, definitely yes, I definitely do.'

'And what attracts you to her?'

'She is a lost soul.'

'Like yourself.'

'Exactly!'

'And two lost souls equal …?'

'One found soul.'

'Redemption through a woman who is not redeemed herself, an unlikely scenario.'

'I am very hopeful.'

'Have the two lost souls spoken?'

'Not as yet, we are hedging around the subject.'

'Is she is aware of you?'

'In a sense.'

'Where?'

'On a park bench, every day at ten o'clock.'

'Which is in fifteen minutes.'

'Yes, I would like you to come with me. Obviously you being on a fast will help enormously, heightened perception and all that.'

'I'll do my best.'

'Excellent, and now to my rendez-vous.'

We left the café. The day was warming up, the trees swaying in the faint breeze. We walked down the steps to the canal. The water was moving slowly, a layer of oil on the top where a duck and her three ducklings, growing up now, but who we had known since they were merely balls of fluff, were gliding down towards the lock. We had had a competition in the office as to what their names should be. It had been a close run thing and had been decided through a very involved voting process, whittling down a myriad of choices to the pharaohs Khufu, Khafre and Menkaure.

We called out our greetings to our duckie friends and then hurried to the rendez-vous.

'I have to be here first,' whispered Tim.

'Why?' I whispered back.

'Because that is how it has always been. We have our established rituals and woe betide the day they are broken.'

I smiled, somewhat unconvincingly, in agreement. However, I was intrigued to see what this mysterious woman looked like. So many possibilities, ranging from a bag lady to an Arabian princess who escaped her household every day for ten minutes.

'You mustn't be seen,' whispered Tim.

That was a quandary. It was a toss up between perching

up a tree or hiding behind the cabin of the houseboat. I chose the boat.

'I'll give you a whistle when you can come out.'

Tim was looking positively ridiculous as he sat in a posed, relaxed fashion on the bench. On the other hand, I felt rather stupid clambering onto the boat, trying not to trip on the ropes.

I hadn't considered there'd be anyone on board. So easy to forget these obvious things, but once I was on the other side of the cabin I could see a girl and a guy lying on a bed.

So, not the right choice, back to the tree, but a woman was now approaching Tim's bench. So I stayed, feeling ridiculous, and hungry! I really shouldn't have agreed to go for a walk, let alone do anything so precarious on an empty stomach.

The woman sat down beside Tim, not even on the end of the bench, but right beside him, as though they knew each other. Both stared straight ahead in their separate universes. I couldn't tell much, she had dark hair, seemingly attractive, probably mid thirties, maybe younger, pretty sure not older, wearing trendy dark glasses so no chance of picking her out of a police line-up. Tim was staunch, he didn't move a muscle and appeared to be intensely interested in the tree across the water. And below me I could smell bacon. Can you believe it? Bacon! And of course they were naked. I had to catch a glimpse, unbelievably gorgeous, some sort of bohemian wonderland, bound to be poets.

How long until this woman left and I could escape the scent of bacon?

There was a knocking on the cabin window. The couple

had seen me.

There were lots of possibilities. Best just to smile and act normally. My primary goal was for Tim's silent companion not to notice me.

'Hello,' I said, cheerfully.

'Hi!' they both said, standing there, obviously aware of how beautiful they were, never been jealous in their lives.

'Have you had breakfast?' the guy asked.

'No, I'm on a fast.'

'Wow, cool,' said the girl, appearing genuinely impressed. 'What about coffee, or a drink, come on in.'

Tim was still sitting there motionless and I decided I would see better from inside.

'My friend asked me to spy on him.'

'The guy on the bench?' asked the girl, pulling a shirt over her head.

'He's met this woman.'

'Who he's never talked to.'

'Exactly. You've been watching him?'

'It's hard not to, he's been here every day for the last couple of weeks. My name's Andrew.'

'Charles.'

'Jess.'

'American?'

'Boston.'

'Ah.'

'Like some coffee?'

'Absolutely,' I replied, sitting down, feeling more comfortable now they were both dressed.

'Is there anything you can tell me about the woman?'

'She always wears black, looks straight ahead and doesn't answer her cell phone.'

'We've been making up all kinds of scenarios,' said Andrew, handing me the coffee.

'We were thinking of inviting them for a drink but they're so intriguing it seems a shame to ruin their time together.'

'So they've never spoken?'

'They haven't even looked at each other.'

Jess flicked the bacon onto plates.

'Now we're going to tempt you! How long is your fast and is it more important than bacon?'

That made me ponder. I still wasn't completely sure what I was aiming to achieve, just the vague concept of clarity, not like the pain in my stomach that cramped in recognition of food.

'Not sure,' I said, looking away from the plates. 'Something to do with getting my thoughts straight.'

'And is it working?'

'I only started this morning.'

I caught a glimpse of movement out of the corner of my eye as the bacon loomed enticingly closer.

'Looks like my friend is off,' I smiled. 'Thanks for the coffee.'

'Drop by anytime, perhaps after you've finished your fast.'

'I'll do that,' I said, climbing out of the boat, looking to the right at the woman striding away. Then I jumped back onto the pathway.

'Enjoyed yourself?' asked Tim.

'Immensely,' I replied. 'What about you, any progress?'

'I think so, yes.'

'But no words.'

'Not as such.'

'Any possibility of words?'

'Yes,' he nodded, slowly. 'Sooner rather than later, I suspect.'

Then we turned and followed the canal back to work.

Chapter Two

Tim and I had a drink after work at his place. I wasn't sure it was intelligent to drink on a very empty stomach, but it was good to feel something inside me.

'I know where she lives,' proclaimed Tim, swirling the red wine in his glass.

'You're a stalker!'

'No, I merely look out my window, and there she is.'

'Where?'

Tim pointed to one of the flats opposite.

'There, and in exactly two minutes she will be home.'

'You're worrying me.'

'She intrigues me. When you read a book you don't put it down just because it intrigues you.'

'A valid argument if a book were a person.'

'Just watch.'

The door opened and the woman entered the flat. She took off her shoes and disappeared into another room.

'Thirty two seconds,' said Tim.

We waited, both of us looking at our watches, and exactly thirty two seconds later she reappeared, changed into sweat pants and top.

'Wine.'

She walked across to the fridge, opened it, got out a bottle of white wine, poured it into a glass and took a sip.

'Microwave.'

She reached into the freezer, extracted a frozen dinner,

unwrapped it and put it in the microwave.

She stared at the microwave until it had finished, then took out the dinner, put it on a plate, put the plate onto a tray, sat down on a couch, picked up a remote control and pointed it at the TV.

'Wine.'

She put the tray back down, stood up, retrieved her wine from the bench and sat down again.

'And that's it, she just sits there till 10.30 and goes to bed.'

'Every night?'

'I don't know, I'm not here every night, but when I've been here this is what happens.'

'It's so sad.'

'Yet so beautiful.'

'We must do something.'

'Of course.'

'Any ideas?'

'I have considered sending her flowers.'

'So simple, so endearing, yet so common.'

'Perhaps a flowering cactus?'

'Original, yet hardly likely to have the desired effect.'

'Then what?'

'I don't know.'

We decided I should return and study the subject for the next few nights, which I did, Tim and I gazing at her as she went through her slow, meaningless ritual.

Friday night, under the influence of a particularly robust Shiraz, an idea finally came to me.

'Goldfish.'

'Yes,' murmured Tim, looking for some cheese in the

pantry.

'She needs a goldfish.'

'Does she indeed?' asked Tim, breaking off a large chunk of camembert. 'That's certainly an unusual idea. Is it based on anything in particular, or have you just been trying to come up with the most unlikely scenario?'

'It is based on the quest of a lonely woman looking for companionship, and the rather elongated courtship by the anonymous spy across the courtyard.'

'Then a goldfish it shall be.'

'Tomorrow the goldfish shall triumph. Have you got any more of that wine?'

Chapter Three

The next day I woke early, immediately aware of the pain in my stomach. No food, still no food, this was only supposed to last two days and here I was at the end of the week, in pain and slightly hallucinating.

I sat up slowly, my head floating behind me, my limbs unsteady. I was going to discover something and I knew the goldfish would lead me to it. I walked gingerly to the shower and let the pounding water stir my mind. It was an important day, the day I was going to merge two lives together with the help of a goldfish.

It was sunny outside. I walked slowly, the light playing tricks on my eyes. The edges of the buildings were etched as though the painter had discarded the watercolour of the past few months and picked up a sharp pencil, determining exactly where one shape started and another finished.

The tree on the corner was swishing in the breeze, the light speckling onto the pavement. I had a sudden urge to touch the shadows of the leaves, to discover the meaning of their patterns.

'No no, don't do it just because you're hungry,' I could hear someone say from behind me, but there was no one there.

I knelt and ran my hand over the grain of the paving stones, exploring the depths of the cracks between them as the patterns of the leaves ran over me and the combination of shadow and light flickered about my face and caught in my eyes. I was mesmerised, amazed, part of me knowing this was ridiculous, another part of me believing that I could feel the earth breathing, that the wind from the four corners of the world was entering me, the light from a million miles away was piercing my eyes, the patterns were bringing clarity. Here then was truth, a moment of revelation, instant connection with that which was and always would be.

A truck rumbled slowly nearer, a dark shadow, the oppressing noise of a dying civilisation.

A man jumped out.

'Want a hand?'

To say yes, to say no, to say nothing, to say everything ...

'Here you go.'

He lifted me up and dropped me on a seat outside the corner store.

I smiled, a little too much.

'Take care,' said the man, a big guy wearing a black top and jeans.

I waved, at least I think I did. There was something wrong. Was it that I should still be lying on the pavement letting the wonders of the world pass over and through me, or was it that I shouldn't be lying on the pavement at all?

'Mustn't lie on the pavement,' I murmured. 'Must find goldfish.'

That was it! It was the day of the goldfish, a day of love, of two lives coming together because of me.

I felt energised and walked quickly up the road towards the pet shop.

So many people were wandering around, lots of them going into M&S, a place that sold food, something I needed, obviously needed, I couldn't keep going like this. Yet I must, onwards, onwards and upwards, the pet shop wasn't far away, just around the corner, but which corner, this one or the next one or the one after that?

'The next one,' I said loudly, startling the woman with her trolley walking towards me.

I didn't bother apologising. I had to conserve energy to get to the pet shop.

And there it was, just as I had pictured it, with bunnies curled up sleeping, waiting for the daily prodding and banging on the windows. What a life, lying there hoping someone might love them, how desperate is that? I darted into the shop to grab the bunnies and run to the park, to set them free from their dreadful little cages. But the sight of all the goldfish in tanks along the wall stopped me, focussed my thoughts.

I had to choose one.

Just one.

I stood, floundering, as such, in front of the hundreds of fish. Now the time had come to choose one, I wasn't sure I was up to the task. Several hundred fish and I had to choose one, but not just any one, one that would change the lives of two people. It couldn't be an ordinary fish. No, no, this had to be the right fish.

'Can I help you?' asked a particularly pretty girl in a green top.

'Yes, maybe you can. I am looking for a fish that will bring two lonely people together.'

'Not a common request,' she smiled.

'These aren't common people. They are quite

extraordinary on both the inside and the outside, so I require an extraordinary fish.'

'I'll show you my favourite,' she ventured, still smiling, but seeming to take my quest seriously.

'This one,' she said, pointing to what I could only describe as a pure goldfish, gold all over with a slim body. 'I love its eyes.'

'Do you just?'

I ventured closer, my nose touching the glass, searching to see if it had that certain quality.

'Would you like it?'

'Would I?'

Perhaps I would, perhaps I wouldn't. I didn't know, didn't have a clue.

'I'm sure it's the right fish for love.'

I turned, my eyes meeting hers, bright, full of light, the sort of eyes you should trust, so I did.

'Yes, please,' I said enthusiastically, and stood back while she put it into a plastic bag.

'Here you go.'

I paused.

'Shouldn't I pay you?'

'Not for such a special fish. There are some things you shouldn't pay for. Like a four leafed clover ...'

She smiled as I remembered. She had been the girl on the bike.

'Oh, yes, yes, sorry, I didn't recognise you. Thank you for the fish ... and the clover ... and ...'

I apologised again and quickly left the shop. It was time to find Tim.

He was asleep, of course, being Saturday. So I banged loudly on the door and threw stones at his window.

'Tim!'

There was a clattering as the window opened and his bedraggled, and one has to say, not at all attractive head, appeared at the window.

'What?'

'I have the fish!'

He blinked.

'The fish!'

He stared at me as though I were a madman.

'The fish!'

He didn't move.

'Just open the door.'

Still no movement.

'Open the door!'

He disappeared inside. There was a short wait and then the door opened.

'And put on some clothes!'

He recognised his nakedness and retreated back up the stairs.

I wandered into the kitchen and poured myself some fruit juice.

I put the fish down gently on the bench, giving it a friendly wave, it was after all going to be the star of the day.

There was the thumping of Tim descending the stairs.

'What are you and that fish doing at my place at 9.30 on a Saturday morning?' Tim asked, pushing past me to the coffee machine.

'Today you are going to fall in love.'

He turned and stared at me, then continued preparing the coffee.

I decided it was safest to leave him to it, and, feeling rather faint from all my walking, I took up residence on his couch.

The coffee machine churned and steamed, filling the room with a delicious smell. I closed my eyes momentarily and dreamed of when I had travelled to Morocco in search of a woman who had sent us an alluring book about painting with spices. She had refused to fall in love with me despite my best intentions.

'Who am I going to fall in love with?'

Tim was sitting on a chair eating breakfast, his coffee finished.

'The girl you stare at every night, of course.'

'Today?'

'Yes.'

'So you bought a fish.'

'Yes.'

It all seemed so clear to me, my sleep had done me good.

'She always sits in the park on Saturday mornings, doesn't she?'

'Every Saturday, like clockwork.'

'Then you are going to meet her there this morning and give her the fish.'

'Have you gone completely nuts?'

'No, and I'll tell you why, because the girl who gave me a four leafed clover gave me the goldfish, and she didn't charge me a penny, which means this will be a success.'

Tim ate some toast.

'So we need to leave soon, Tim.'

He licked his finger.

'I'd suggest something casual.'

He stood up.

'So you're coming?'

He yawned and walked to the bench.

'This is the fish?'

'Absolutely. I didn't choose it, the girl …'

'Who gave you a four leafed clover …'

'That's right.'

'You're completely nuts.'

Tim shrugged and headed upstairs.

I waited, wanting to be certain he'd come back down, but somewhat hesitant, starting to mull over what I would do if he didn't.

Another orange juice was in order.

'Let's go then,' said Tim, coming down the stairs.

'Absolutely,' I agreed, picking up the fish, relieved, and excited again.

We walked quickly to the park as the traffic got busier.

'There she is.'

'There she is,' agreed Tim. 'Now what?'

'You sit down next to her, put the goldfish between you, then walk away.'

'Okay.'

Tim did just that.

'Now we go back to your place.'

She duly returned to her flat. We were both at the window, staring on tenterhooks to see if she had the goldfish. And there it was, in her hand. She walked in, put it on the kitchen bench, then left.

We turned to each other, Tim questioningly, me shrugging. I didn't know how this was going to pan out.

She returned twenty minutes later with a large plastic bag out of which she took a bowl, half filled it with water, poured in some pebbles and draped some oxygen weed on top of the water. Then she poured the water and the fish from the plastic bag very slowly, carefully, into the bowl, placed it on her coffee table and stared at it for five minutes.

'Success!' I proclaimed, not sure why, but I sounded very positive.

'Why?' asked Tim.

'You just wait for Monday night,' I said, again with no idea why I was saying what I was saying.

'Monday night will reveal all. I'll see you then.'

I left Tim, baffled, torn between staring at the girl staring at the fish, and his now obviously insane friend, who descended the stairs with a wave of his hand, all smiles.

I wasn't particularly sure about walking. My head was rather woozy and my legs were slightly shaking, so I had to devise a plan to keep this fast going, at least till Monday night when all would be revealed. I owed it to myself not to give up now. Ideas were coming into my head that were completely original, ones I would never have had without fasting. Perhaps I was reaching my epiphany. Maybe soon I would discover something of myself or the world that would change both of us forever.

I definitely couldn't keep walking. I sat down to devise a plan. What could I do for two and a half days that didn't involve physical effort or sitting by myself either at home or on the pavement?

Perhaps I needed another form of transport. A car? No, I would drive off the road. A bus, no, a train, maybe, a plane? Now there was an idea. I could travel round the world. No, no, no, seriously crazy. But the more I lingered on the thought, the more I liked it. All I needed was a travel agent and some money. Well, I had money, so I had to find a travel agent. This shouldn't be too hard I told myself as I lurched to my feet, the ache in my stomach increasing as I stood up.

'This is completely stupid!'

I don't think the words came out of my mouth. No one reacted, the girl beside me kept walking.

I tried again.

'This is completely stupid!'

I was sure I had said something but no one took any notice of me.

I kept walking, ridiculously slowly, people almost hitting me.

The door of the travel agent appeared like an oasis in the desert. I attempted to appear nonchalant, knowing that I wasn't looking my best.

'Morning,' I said, casually, confidently.

'Hi there,' said a girl, smiling, possibly with an Australian accent.

'I thought I'd buy a ticket.'

'Where to?'

'Well, I'm not sure. I need to go a long way away, perhaps New Zealand?'

'Great country.'

'Great, great country.'

'When did you want to go?'

'Today.'

That was a bit sudden, one didn't travel across the world on a whim. Her look changed. I had become a lunatic in her eyes. Perhaps they had a panic button, perhaps she was reaching for it now and in a moment the police would arrive asking all sorts of questions and locking me up. That wouldn't work. I had to be at Tim's on Monday night when all was going to be revealed. I just had to make it to Monday night.

'Tell you what, perhaps I won't go after all.'

'Are you sure?'

'Yes, yes, some things are better not rushed. I'll come back another day.'

I turned to go, slightly losing balance. I looked like a drunk. No one would believe I was on a fast, probably wouldn't know what a fast was. Did I? Yes, absolutely, I was starving, really really starving. Time to go home.

Time to go home, time to go, time ...

Someone was talking to me, saying something pleasant, perhaps offering me something delicious to eat.

'What is your name?'

'Charles.'

'Charles, we're taking you to hospital.'

I opened my eyes. There was a man in a uniform looking professionally concerned.

'Do you always look like that?'

'Can you focus?'

'You drive an ambulance?'

'Yes I do, Charles.'

'I'd really rather go home.'

'I think you should come with us.'

'No, I've got to make sure, I've got to, I've got …'

Sitting up in hospital, I felt remarkably healthy. Focussed, alert, all body parts moving.

'You're awake?'

'Yes I am,' I replied, to the ridiculously attractive nurse.

'You're very lucky. Not even a broken bone.'

'I'm on a fast.'

'That would explain a lot.'

'So why am I here?'

'You don't remember?'

'I remember a very concerned ambulance man.'

'You were hit by a car, actually three cars.'

'Three?'

'From all accounts it was a game of pinball on the High Street.'

'I remember going to the travel agent.'

'Then you walked straight out onto the street.'

'Crikey!'

'Exactly!'

'So what now?'

'Stay here for a few tests. They should let you out on Wednesday.'

'That could be a problem, I have to be at a friend's Monday evening.'

'It is Monday evening.'

I smiled, disbelieving.

'What time?'

'Five thirty.'

'I'll be just in time.'

'For what?'

'I haven't really got time to explain.'

'You can't leave.'

'Have to, I'm afraid. Something to do with love and a goldfish.'

'No, seriously, you can't, we need to do a lot more tests.'

'Of course you do, lots more checks. What would you prefer? I could send you away for a cup of water and then make a dash for it? Or we could just be adults and you could help me leave. I'll be back in a couple of hours, no one will know.'

'I'd be in so much trouble.'

'Yes, but you can't refuse a pinball victim a glass of water.'

I smiled, she smiled.

'Just pretend it's a movie.'

'Tell you what, Charles, if you can make it out of hospital in the state you're in, you'll probably pass the tests.'

She left the room very professionally, opening a cupboard as she went where my clothes had been neatly hung. I stood up, enjoyed the light-headedness, shut the door, got dressed and then sauntered along the corridor, down the lifts, and out into the sun speckled beauty of a London evening.

'Taxi!'

I got in, sat back, and enjoyed the combined exhilaration of escaping from the hospital and the anticipation of seeing Tim and the girl.

'Thanks!' I called, watching the taxi briefly as it drove

away. Then I turned to knock on Tim's door.

'Charles!'

'Tim!'

'Where have you been? I've been ringing all over town.'

'Hospital.'

'Are you all right?'

'Apparently not.'

'What happened?'

'There's no time to discuss that now!'

We were just in time to see the mystery woman's front door open. She looked normal, everything was normal, except she was carrying an M&S plastic bag, and when she closed the door she walked straight to the kitchen, put down the bag, opened the pantry, got out a small packet, and sprinkled it over the goldfish bowl.

'Ah!' sighed Tim.

She went to her bedroom and came back in track pants and a t-shirt and emptied the bag of its vegetables and a packet of meat.

'Aha!'

We both watched, spellbound, as she cooked dinner, talking all the while to the goldfish.

Then she sat down with dinner at the table, still talking to the goldfish that swam in front of her.

'A goldfish,' whispered Tim, 'Who would have guessed? A goldfish!'

'A goldfish,' I agreed, nodding, now feeling rather weak.

'We should celebrate.'

'We should, absolutely, but I have to get back to the hospital. I did promise the nurse.'

Tim looked very concerned.

'They say it's nothing. I got a little distracted being on a fast so I walked into some cars, or they drove into me, one of the two, but they say I'm fine, they just want to check.'

'I'd better take you.'

'Yes, I'm not sure I can get there on my own.'

'Come on then.'

Sitting in Tim's car, I felt like I had been on a very long journey.

'I think I'll talk to her tomorrow,' he said.

'You must.'

'Yes, I must.'

There was a long silence, filled with the sounds of passing traffic.

'Are you going to keep fasting?'

'No, Monday night, I made it to Monday night. Achieved goals, and tomorrow ...'

'Tomorrow?'

'Tomorrow is up to you.'

The nurse was pleasantly surprised to see me. She told me off appropriately in front of her superior, then tucked me into bed.

'I have to be gone by nine tomorrow morning, just to warn you.'

'I'll schedule the tests for tomorrow afternoon. Can you get back by then?'

'Absolutely, good night.'

'Good night Charles.'

I fell asleep, certain in my delirious state that she was overwhelmingly in love with me.

Chapter Four

It was much more difficult to sneak out of a hospital at nine o'clock, but I was feeling great having ended my fast, and they had hooked me up during the night to all sorts of nutrients that dripped into my veins.

So many plans flashed through my brain, so many images of TV and film escapes. But this was the real thing. It had to be simple and effective. I didn't want a dozen nurses running after me while I ripped out the drip and dashed into a taxi. As it was, it was ridiculously simple. I put on my clothes, waited untill the nurses were sitting in their station, and walked out. Bit of an anticlimax, there was even a taxi waiting outside that took me to Camden Lock.

I was early and there was the smell of bacon cooking in the house boat. I knocked on a window and the girl's face appeared. Yes she was naked, didn't bother to hide it.

'Charles.'

Darn it, she remembered my name. It put the pressure on me. I was completely useless with names. I had a feeling it was Jess, certain his name was Andrew, Jess and Andrew, Andrew and Jess, did that sound right? Had to give it a go.

'Jess!' I said, confidently.

'Come on in, we're having breakfast. Are you still on a fast?'

'No, I finished last night.'

'Any revelations?' asked Andrew, extending his hand in welcome.

'No, but definitely results, and a story for the grandchildren if any come along.'

They quickly put on t-shirts and shorts and dished up the breakfast onto three plates.

'Cheers!' I said, tucking in, gulping it down, then looking up guiltily.

'Don't worry,' laughed Andrew. 'I'll fry up some more and you can tell us about your adventures.'

I tried to say no, but there's no stopping an insistent American, and the food was delicious.

When I had finished, a couple of minutes later, it was almost ten o'clock.

'I'm hoping we'll see something different this morning.'

'The mysterious silent love affair.'

'That may not be so silent.'

'Oooh!'

We crowded around the curtained window, just in time to see the beautifully groomed woman sit down on the chair.

'Now where is he? Where is he?'

I couldn't see Tim.

'Come on Tim, you can do it.'

Still no one on the path.

'Tim!'

He couldn't let me down, not now, not after all I'd been through.

There was a slight thud against the houseboat and we peered out the front to see Tim getting out of a small dinghy.

'Good morning,' he said to the woman. 'My name is Tim. I believe we have met before but not been formally introduced.'

He extended his hand, smiling.

All three of us on the boat held our breath.

She smiled and took his hand.

'Jenny.'

'A pleasure to meet you.'

'Likewise.'

'I have a little morning tea on my boat if you would care to join me?'

'I would very much like that.'

We dashed down to the far end of the houseboat as Tim helped her onto the boat which was laden with roses, a bucket of champagne and a platter of cheese and fruit.

They were laughing and talking and I found myself laughing and hugging Andrew and Jess as Tim pushed off, smiling, being enchanting as only he can.

Chapter Five

Three weeks later I made a sudden decision to catch the tube to Charing Cross and pick up a novel to read. I loved reading old books. I'd spend hours wandering around second-hand bookshops, leafing through the pages, enjoying comments people had written. I'd imagine where they'd been, who they'd been in love with, or fallen out of love with, while they read the book. The spirit of each reader lingered on the pages, sharing a part of themselves with the book.

I stood near the edge of the platform waiting for the rush of air blasting through the tunnels before the train roared past, coming to a stop with a squealing of brakes. People got off, relieved to be heading back towards the surface. I got on and removed a copy of *The Sun* that proclaimed the demise of another politician.

Several sat in the carriage, deep in that neutral state the Tube invokes. Don't look, don't speak, don't acknowledge, it is a place where life stops until the doors open and the world beckons. I sat back, staring at the combination of darkness and random lights flickering past me. Suddenly the front door of the carriage opened and through came two boys and one girl, probably aged around 13 or 14. Immediately they smiled, bright flashes of light, their eyes gleaming as they introduced themselves in thick Eastern European accents. Then they began playing the piano accordion, violin and mouth organ.

I couldn't help but smile. What a fantastic racket, but so enjoyable. I clapped along, encouraging them, ignoring the scowls from the other passengers around me.

Then we were coming into the station and before you could blink they were putting their caps out to the passengers, a couple of whom grudgingly gave them money. I only had a £10 note. I handed it over enthusiastically.

'Brilliant!' I said to the girl, who gave me a kiss on the cheek.

Then they were gone, off to another carriage, leaving the beat of their music playing in my head. I got off the train and walked along the tunnels. There were a couple more buskers. One was a guitar player, wonderful, Argentinean from the looks of him, strumming as though the guitar pumped the blood through his veins. The other was a saxophone player, perhaps West Indian, playing long slow lingering notes. I walked slower, enjoying it, then forced myself to go back up towards the light of the world filled with busy people and their busy lives.

The girl at the bookshop had glasses, pigtails, a vintage sort of top and stammered a little, so where else was she going to fit in so incredibly well? She was defined by her smile. Whenever someone came to the counter she smiled and her eyes lit up as though the customer was a long lost friend. I'm sure all the guys were completely in love with her and asked all sorts of questions in which they had no interest. They couldn't help it, they just had to let that extraordinary smile permeate their being before they headed back to work. It increased sales too which wasn't lost on management, especially in a business where every penny counts.

'Hi Mel.'

'Charles!' she replied, as though we'd had dinner the night before. 'How's business?'

'Never been better.'

'Great! Let me know if I can find anything for you.'

'Will do,' I said, turning away.

I wasn't at all sure what I was after, there were so many choices. It was fun looking through books in which I had absolutely no interest, such as gardening. An odd thing to spend hours on. The world didn't need a gardener, the chaos of natural birth and death created a balance of perfect beauty, and yet there were dozens of books on how to manipulate what was an adequate natural event into an unnatural cultivated thing. For what purpose? To make things orderly, but then they lost their beauty. It is in the ramblings of the natural world that one discovers the wonders of beauty. As they say, a perfectly symmetrical face is not beautiful, it is in the non symmetrical, the unexpected, the slight dent in a nose, a mole, the wrinkle when a girl smiles, the slightly different coloured eyes, the hair that blows randomly in the wind, the tripping of a girl on the footpath and her smile when she recovers herself.

I moved on to historical battles, to the lives of those who made themselves famous by killing more people than anyone else. Past the art books, to the biographies of poets. Now here was the imperfect. How could a poet possibly live a controlled, exact, ordered life? The French poets who had discovered the utter meaninglessness of life amidst the extraordinary beauty of the North African coast, who had immersed themselves in Parisienne life so that they saw through all hope and reached hopelessness, who had delved into the wonders of the human mind only to discover that nothing had any meaning, that ennui pervaded the root of all. To live or not to live, to kill or not to kill, to discover beauty or be tormented by beauty. Nothing was of any meaning, all was vanity.

On to the novels. Durrell caught my eye immediately with his distinctively awful covers that summoned the reader to acknowledge the sheer brilliance of literature and of life lost in Alexandria. The characters were etched forever in the memories of the readers who dwelt there, never leaving that extraordinary land.

A girl was standing, looking at the shelf in a definitive way, as though she could see through the covers and into the books. She carefully made a selection. Her fingers plucked Durrell's *Clea* from the shelf and, without opening the pages, she went straight to the counter.

I stopped for a moment, mesmerised. There was something about the girl. Was it because she was a girl, a good enough reason to stop at any time, or was it more, was there something I had sensed, that I shouldn't miss? Did I know her, had I met her, been introduced, merely sat on a train opposite her?

She paid for the book and left, out into the sunshine, and I had to follow her, yes, had to, no choice. There's some things you've just got to do, you can't let go past.

She headed towards the National Gallery. I hurried after her, dodging people moving like heat seeking missiles back to work, why I'll never know. How many of them enjoy their jobs? I love mine and I still only linger back to the office.

I just about took out a whole Japanese tour party as I passed through the doors, looking frantically to catch her up. There she was, climbing the stairs, not too far away. I lengthened my stride, suddenly wondering what her name might be. Was she English, not very likely. Mind you, what is English nowadays? English is pretty well any nationality on the globe. So let's narrow it down. European, probably Eastern. Polish? Hungarian? No, Romanian, that was it, Romanian.

She had stopped. I almost missed her. I was going a bit fast for my own good, sort of like my mind, off in its own world, speeding along, thinking all sorts of things had happened, but in fact they were merely whims of my fancy. Not a problem if you're at a pub or wandering in the countryside, but at the office it was a little disconcerting when I thought glorious publishing deals had gone through, but they had only occurred in my mind.

So there she was, standing in a large high ceilinged room. I sat down on a black leather chair trying to look nonchalant but thoroughly, totally absorbed, becoming more and more amazed by her.

How could I not be drawn into her world? She was like a work of art yet not static, dead, like the art around her that relied on human spirits to bring them to life within their minds. She was alive, every detail as clearly defined as a winter landscape, unmoving, yet incredibly fluid.

I sat watching, as absorbed in her as she was in the painting, van Gogh's *Three Figures Near A Canal With Windmill*. Now I could stop and take in her details. Her jeans were ripped, her hair was roughly cropped, her shirt crumpled.

She appeared to be gradually, almost imperceptibly, merging into the painting. She moved closer and closer until she seemed in my mind to become one of the painted figures lost amidst the bleak landscape. The brushstrokes of her form were broad and vivid, searching for the revelation that was promised beyond that far off horizon. She looked back at me, her dark eyes discovering more than I wanted to reveal. I glanced away, alarmed, then she turned abruptly and walked briskly to the exit.

I had to make an instant decision. To follow her or to return to work.

I followed, certain she could sense me close behind, desperate not to lose her now I had made my decision, the traffic roaring about us and pedestrians dashing from one side of the road to the other.

She entered Leicester Square tube station, almost running down the stairs, past the beggars who pathetically asked for money, long since having lost their shame amidst their desperation to eat.

I stood so close behind her in the ticket queue I could see the hairs on the back of her neck as we paid for our tickets, one to Mornington Crescent I heard her say. Then down the escalators and into the airless dank atmosphere of the platform.

She walked slowly now, giving me time to catch up, to stand nearby. The wind from the oncoming train blew against our faces, forcing the pollution into our lungs. Then the doors opened and we got on the same carriage, me sitting a few seats down from her, watching her reflection.

The train screeched to a stop at Mornington Crescent, a station that had been closed for many years where ghost stories abounded. Only three of us got off and entered the same lift. I snuck several glances at the girl beside me as the lift rose, but she remained staring at the steel doors.

Outside, she went straight to a corner store. I can recall every single detail as though it was in front of me now, the different smells and the stock on the shelves with their white sticky price labels.

The girl went up to the counter and her lips creased into a tired smile.

'I need some money please.'

The man in his 50s, Asian, with a darkness under his eyes, looked up from the Daily Mirror newspaper he was reading.

Neither spoke for a moment.

'I need some money please,' she said again, with that same voice, that same sad smile.

'I do not have much to give,' said the man.

'I understand,' she said, almost imperceptibly, the vibrations of her voice mingling with the rumblings of a passing truck.

'Fifty pounds is all I need,' she whispered. 'You will still have enough for your children.'

There was another pause.

'Fifty pounds? Yes, yes, I can give you fifty pounds. Here …'

He fumbled with the till, opened it, and gave her a wad of notes.

'Thank you,' she said quietly. 'I am very sorry. Life is not easy for any of us.'

With that she turned and walked past, not giving me a glance. I followed her, avoiding the shopkeeper, keeping my head down.

Back in the street the girl crossed to the other side and ducked up an alley, past the old lady selling second hand clothes who smiled at her.

We hurried by the terraced houses and the small shops, one roasting its own coffee, filling the air with a rich aroma. Then into Sainsbury's where she guided a trolley slowly round the aisles, selecting the items on a crumpled list and paying for them with the fifty pounds from the shop.

We left and walked back into the heart of Camden, turning right into a concrete lane. There she stopped and turned, looking directly at me.

'Now we will wait here.'

Immediately she sat on a step, gesturing for me to join her. We remained there silently for two hours as humanity passed us by. Every single person was different. Their bodies, clothes, hair, the look in their eyes, their personalities, the way they walked confidently or shuffled. Some were proud, others avoided my eye. Many were wrapped up in themselves, paying no attention to the world about them. There were so many different English accents, so many from other parts of the globe. We sat there, without talking or eating for two hours, immersed in the wonder of this tiny space, so seemingly insignificant in passing, and yet for two hours it became our world.

Then they came, one at a time most of them. Old men, staggering, clutching their beer cans, Fosters and Guinness, occasionally one or two with spirits, some hiding them when they saw the girl, but often too late. They stank, reeking of dirt and urine. Their clothes were too big for them, held up by string or an old belt.

As each of them arrived, the girl stood and greeted them by name, smiling, chatting, as though they were old friends. I listened to their conversations, about who they had met, what their friends had done, their problems with the police and social services. Others, particularly the older men, could only mumble incoherently. Then she gave them a hug and slipped an item from her shopping into their pockets.

Finally a man came, taller than most, and younger. His clothes appeared less worn, as though he had bought them when they were new. The girl went up to him, just like the others, extending her hands in embrace, making herself vulnerable as she hugged him firmly.

She reached into her bag and gave him something. He took it, the gold ring on his finger standing out in the grim concrete surroundings.

His eyes lingered over hers.

'Thank you,' he murmured, opening his arms to hold her once more, and as he did so his right hand reached round her and a knife appeared.

Chapter Six

The world stopped, nothing moved. The birds, people, even the wind. Everything in that small corridor of the world came to an instant halt.

I couldn't breathe. I wanted to. I screamed internally at my lungs to work, but no air came into me. I couldn't move and nor could anyone else. We could only look from one horrified person to another as the girl lay there, blood now coming from beneath her and staining the pavement.

Her eyes were open but she knew it was the last time she would see us. It was the end. She smiled, then closed her eyes. It was then that the air came rushing back into our lungs and we leapt forward to help. A couple worked valiantly to revive her, but she had gone.

Some began to cry, then to weep. A couple of the old guys slumped to the ground in despair. People started coming from everywhere. They all knew her, she had been a part of their world. The hostels in the area were emptied as staff and residents flooded into the alley. Dozens, then hundreds, all participating in grief for the girl.

I stood back. I had only been a part of her world for such a short time, a moment in her history. How old was she? How long had she been doing this? Did she rob shops every day to get the money to feed the poor?

I wanted to ask someone, to find out more, but there was no one who seemed detached enough to talk, they were all filled with grief.

They gathered there, laying her gently on a tattered piece of cloth. The police arrived and they too knew her, understood what was happening, and joined in the memorial to this extraordinary girl. Then the priest from the Catholic church stood up from where he had been kneeling beside the girl and whispered to a few of the men. They gently picked her up and carried her at the head of an impromptu procession to the Catholic church.

I followed amongst the crowd which was growing larger as word spread. I hesitated at the church door. I wasn't a Catholic, but an old man touched my arm and indicated he would show me what to do. I made the sign of the cross and bowed, feeling a little disconcerted at how much this meant to so many, and then took a seat.

We sat still, silent, it's hard to describe, it seems so impossible now, to have just sat there in silence, the only utterances being muffled weeping and the coughing of the old folk. My brain was empty. There were no questions, no criticisms, no analysis of the church and their beliefs. I just sat there without moving.

Then they held a mass. I listened to the words, but not as words, more as music, lingering, floating amongst them. In so many years of working, surrounded by words, this was the first time I had experienced words being actually alive. They shared them like one shares air, breathing them in and out, knowing them off by heart. Not just the words but all the different intonations and when to stand and when to sit, finally ending with them queuing in lines towards the altar where they stopped, briefly, before turning with a look in their eyes that held a strange sort of peace.

I left them then. I needed to get away, to discover more of the girl, to make sense of those few hours.

I went to the shop. The man was standing at the counter. I should have been afraid, worried that the police might recognise me, but nothing filled my mind except the girl and the hundreds whose lives she had affected so intimately.

I selected a chocolate bar and put it down on the counter.

The man looked up. Did he recognise me?

'Forty pence, please.'

I gave him the money silently.

'Thank you,' he replied, returning to the paper he was reading.

I just stood there.

'Can I get you anything else?' he asked.

'Yes, please,' I hesitated.

What was I doing, why was I there? This man had been the victim of a robbing this morning, I should just let him be.

'What would you like?'

'I was wondering if you knew anything about the girl who robbed you this morning?' I asked.

He looked at me, puzzled.

'I was not robbed this morning.'

'She took fifty pounds.'

'You are mistaken.'

I took a step back, thinking I should just leave.

'Are you the police?'

'No, no, it's just that I was here, this morning.'

'Oh, I see.'

'And she was killed.'

'Antya was killed?'

'You know her?'

'Of course, everyone knows her. She is our angel.'

'She was killed.'

He paused.

'You must be mistaken.'

'I was there. A man used a knife.'

'But she is our angel, she cannot die.'

'I'm very sorry.'

The man leaned heavily against the counter.

'Where is she now?'

'I was at a mass.'

'She is in the church?'

'I think she still is, I presume so.'

'Then I must go to her. I must go. Excuse me, I'm very sorry.'

He reached for his keys.

'I'm very sorry, but I must go.'

He opened the door for me to leave and then hurried past me up the road, shaking his head as he went, meeting others on the footpath as they headed for the church.

I was a complete outsider. These people shared a common love for this girl, one that I couldn't share with them, but to see so many affected so deeply, people who would let themselves be robbed to give money to her cause, what was behind it, who was she, where had she come from, did anyone know, did they all think of her as an angel?

I got on the tube and headed back to the art gallery. I climbed the stairs slowly, remembering each detail of Antya. Then I entered the room where the painting hung. There was no one there, just the memory of the darkness of her eyes. I approached the painting, hesitantly, searching, and then I stopped, a few feet away, and that's where I stayed, now lost in the three characters who were walking away from me over the vast landscape towards the horizon.

There was something mysterious, other worldly about these characters. Perhaps they were evil, bringing desolation upon this already desperate world. No, that would be too awful. But there was no light, no joy about them. They were as desperate, as dark as the landscape. They were heading for the light but they weren't a part of the light, they were merely struggling towards it. Struggling towards the light. As are we all …as are we all … but we're not, we're just not, not all. Maybe a few, maybe those I saw this morning.

Moving so incredibly slowly, struggling, desperately, towards the light amidst the darkness and the shadows.

The characters in the painting seemed to move, slowly, so incredibly slowly, towards the horizon. But I wasn't a part of their journey, I didn't even want to be. I was nothing to do with them, I didn't understand the first thing about what they were trying to achieve, why they were doing it, what it was about. And yet that girl did. She had stood there and became one with those people and the terrifyingly bleak landscape, and had been killed. And hundreds of people had rushed to see her, to respect her as she lay in that church. They had shared their words of life around her as she lay there, a corpse, mourned by so many. And I was nothing to do with it, there was nothing within me that could relate to this picture or to her life and death.

Chapter Seven

I woke up early the next morning. It was another gorgeous day and I couldn't help but feel good. I had breakfast and headed off to work, getting there before anyone else. I made some coffee, always fun with the steam bubbling. I often thought of making the world's largest espresso machine and pouring an unbelievably huge cup of coffee.

I walked through to my office and sat down at the desk. There were lots of books sitting around, manuscripts, tons of letters from authors wanting something or other, emails a plenty and invitations to this and that. There wasn't any chance of getting anything done in such a muddle so I spent ten minutes scooping everything up and dumping it in the corner. Then after a couple of minutes of flicking through my emails I realised it would take me at least half the day to clear them, so I selected all and hit the delete button. Some programmer always thinks we haven't made the right choice so a little box asked me if I wanted to do what I had decided to do.

'Of course I do!'

I deleted the deleted items and my inbox was empty just as Tim came through the door.

'Wow!'

'I know, meet Mr Organised.'

'So where is it all?'

'In the corner.'

'Excellent.'

'It's going to be a good day.'

'As always.'

He left and I sat back, almost tipping the chair over. Then I leant forward, sipped the coffee and got some chocolate out of my drawer. It was dark, rich, and apparently good for me, so I often indulged.

Tim peeked round the corner again.

'Want to meet a new author?'

'Interesting?'

'Very'

'Okay.'

'We're having lunch at 12. I'll meet you here and we'll go together.'

That gave me time to go through the pile on the floor. After twenty minutes I stopped, totally uninspired. That annoyed me. I didn't get uninspired at work.

I had to go for a walk. I knew yesterday was getting to me. I'd got a bit emotional and that wasn't a good way to deal with an event, especially a death. I had decided to carry on with life as normal and revisit it in a week or so when I had some objectivity.

I wandered into a bookshop. There were the Top Ten bestsellers with cookbooks beside them and magazines on the shelving. I wandered round looking at the books and glancing at the covers, trying a few of the books lost at the back of the shop, seeing what had been discarded in the sales bin.

Then I found a book on *van Gogh*. Not a good idea really, but it was a fictional account of his early life and, although I had decided to avoid the subject, I couldn't help but buy it.

The woman at the counter said hello, and I said hello, and she took my money and wished me a good day, which was all very pleasant. Then I was off back to work with a small novel in my hand.

I sat down on an armchair on the third floor and opened the book. It was written by Isaac Driver, an American, and published by Auldheim, 2002. Quite recent then.

I delved straight in, not worrying about the introduction by an esteemed university colleague, and I didn't get up again until I heard Tim calling my name.

'Charles, lunch!'

'Lunch.'

'Yes?'

'Yes.'

The author we were supposed to meet was late. The sun poured into the pub which was thoroughly enjoyable, except I wasn't enjoying it.

'What do you know about *van Gogh* that I don't already know?' I asked.

'Not a lot. Pretty standard, sunflowers and all that.'

'Early life?'

'Had an affinity with the poor.'

'Not really your cup of tea?'

'Not at all. If he hadn't cut off his ear I doubt anyone would have bought his work. And his early stuff, absolute crap. Notoriety, that's what you need, except you need it before you die, which was rare for turn of the century artists. Struggled, painted, died miserable deaths. Now sell for millions, we've created a romantic myth. Brilliant marketing. I doubt anyone has a clue how miserable they were. Didn't have enough to eat a lot of the time.'

'I've been thinking about how the poor live.'

'Really?'

'I saw a girl murdered the other day.'

'And she was poor?'

'I don't know, but she helped the poor.'

'Good for her.'

'But we don't do anything for the poor.'

'I give to the Sallies.'

'Is that all?'

'More than most.'

'I was wondering if there was a bit more we could do.'

'Start by reading Marx.'

'It doesn't worry you?'

'Why should it? We live in a country where you can achieve whatever you want, do whatever you want. You can give up and lie on the gutter or you can get off your backside and achieve something. It's a choice, make the decision and live it. But don't expect anyone to pay for your decision.'

He paused, chomping on some salad.

'Charles, I've got to say, a fast and now the poor, what's next, religion? You're not going to be any fun at all in a few weeks.'

It was true. I had to snap out of it.

'Have dinner with Jenny and me this evening.'

'Love to.'

'See you at my place at 8, we'll catch a taxi.'

That afternoon I made myself deliberately busy clearing up my paperwork and didn't think about the girl, or those shabby people, or the church, or *van Gogh*.

I sat back at 6 and admired my ridiculously tidy office. I had a sense of achievement. I was organised for the next while and would get hassled by everyone else in the office for being so tidy.

Tim, Jenny and I headed for Opium, a new restaurant in Soho. It was a great night to be in town. There was a film premiere, the new one by Kate Winslet. Everyone who had made a TV appearance in the last year was walking up the red carpet to Leicester Square where the spotlights were swivelling into the sky.

Dozens of people were crammed against the metal barriers calling out to their favourite stars. The lesser ones walked from the taxis, the more well known ones were chauffeured to the theatre where they got out, waved to the crowds, posed for the photographers, occasionally talked to the wide-eyed girls in the front row, then entered the theatre.

It was also the night of the drummers. There were three different groups around the Square. One was right by the theatre, two guys with braided hair and huge smiles, their hands pounding the drums. Further round by the American ice creams was a group of two drummers, a guitarist, and two girls dancing. They were probably Brazilian, having a great time. A large crowd gathered round them, enjoying their music as much as they were. And just off the square as we headed towards the restaurant were two guys, one with a drum and another with a didgeridoo.

Tim was intrigued.

'Aren't they fantastic instruments?' he called over the

music and the crowd that bustled about us.

'You should give it a go,' I replied.

'Wouldn't have a clue.'

'Go on,' urged Jenny, smiling, tempting.

'Couldn't possibly.'

'Of course you can.'

Jenny walked up to the guy playing the didgeridoo and next thing he was beckoning to Tim.

He tried to ignore him but Jenny grabbed his hand.

'Never played one before,' he protested.

The guy sat him down on the stool.

'Honestly, don't have a clue,' he said, addressing the crowd.

The musician explained how to play the instrument. Tim concentrated, realising there was no way of getting out of it. Then he was handed the long hollow piece of wood and it was Tim's moment of musical reckoning.

'Go Tim!'

He frowned. Then he blew hard.

Nothing came out.

Tim looked up, accusingly, at Jenny and me as he was given some more instructions.

'You can do it darling!'

Tim took a deep breath, blew, and made a noise. It was hard to describe, certainly not what we were expecting, but it was a sound and the crowd cheered.

Tim took that as his cue to leave. He stood, gave a perfunctory bow, then hurried away, leaving us to catch him up.

'I knew you could do it!'

'You knew I'd make a fool of myself.'

'You were fantastic,' laughed Jenny.

'And I'll have none of that from you. I know what's awful and I was truly awful.'

'But you made a sound.'

'Yes I did.'

Jenny took his arm and gave him a kiss on the cheek.

'Yes I did.'

His embarrassment fell away. Jenny was holding him, nothing mattered except for her. He pulled her arm closer.

'Now where is this place?'

Opium was new. It had had rave reviews and was the place to be. It was hard to get a reservation so lucky Tim had connections with the owner. We were shown straight to our table on the fifth floor of terraced seating. There were several more terraces above, dark lighting with candles on the tables, red carpet, lots of dragons, and stars in the dark ceiling.

'Fabulous,' proclaimed Tim.

A waiter, Italian, brought us some champagne compliments of the owner.

'Have you noticed all the waiters are European?'

'Slightly incongruous.'

A violinist and pianist began playing on the stage below us.

'Mozart,' advised Jenny.

'Very popular in the Orient?' I asked.

'Bound to be,' agreed Tim, raising his glass. 'Here's to us!'

'To us!'

It was a fantastic evening, my first real chance to get to

know Jenny who was as wonderful when she spoke as she had been mysteriously silent by the canal. Brought up in New York, she had moved over here for a job with a firm that distributed classical music scores three years go.

We ate and ate, the bottles emptied, there was laughter and enjoyment all around us. Then a jazz group took over the stage and Tim immediately took Jenny's hand and danced, while laughing and whispering in her ear. He was a great dancer and she thoroughly enjoyed herself, complimenting his enthusiasm with a delicate gracefulness. They returned, smiling.

'Coffee?'

'Absolutely.'

We watched the other dancers as we continued talking, exchanging histories, future plans, tidbits from people we had met in our daily lives.

Then eventually we accepted it was time to go. We reluctantly stood, held our chairs to keep us steady, and made our way out.

The streets were filled with people, many of them laughing, some of them singing. It was a great night. The three of us linked arms and wandered around savouring the evening.

Then they came at us from behind a corner with a cash machine. They wore hoods and dark glasses. Other than that I couldn't tell what they looked like except for their height and that they were all guys.

They surrounded us.

'Give us your money,' the shortest one said.

'What?'

'Give us your money, I've got a knife.'

'Really?'

Tim was drunk, he was in a good mood and wasn't able to take them seriously.

'Now!'

'Really, why would you want our money? I've just spent it all at this fantastic new restaurant. You should try it, called Opium, wonderful, the food was extraordinary, not surprised the critics rave about it.'

'Give us your money now!'

'No, really, I've spent it all, haven't got a penny on me. Search my pockets, I gave all my loose change to a delightful young waitress, half as attractive as the lovely lady on my arm, but she brought us food and drink without dropping it on the floor or on our laps and you can't ask for better service than that.'

'Tim!'

'Charles?'

'Let's just give them some money, they've got a knife.'

'Really? I haven't seen any evidence of such an implement.'

'You wanna see my knife?'

'Certainly. There's no point handing over money for no reason. Work hard for it I do, get up every morning, trudge to the office, have to read through a lot of crap before I find the pearl that readers want to read. You should try it for a day, harder than you think.'

'This is your last chance.'

'Here you go,' I said, fumbling in my pocket for some notes.

Tim raised his hand.

'Charles! We're not just handing over money. He hasn't shown us a knife yet. Load of hot air if you ask me. Been watching too much telly, trying to be the big man going round robbing people. Easy option, why don't you find yourself a job instead of play acting? Be a real man!'

The boy whipped his hand out of his pocket and lunged at Tim. Then the three of them turned and ran.

Jenny and I grabbed Tim as he fell to the ground. His eyes were closing and blood was coming out of his shirt.

'Phone an ambulance!' I shouted at Jenny.

I ripped off his shirt exposing the gash, the blood, the mess. I knew I had to apply pressure and pushed down as hard as I could.

'They're coming!'

'Tim, don't close your eyes. Tim! Don't you close your eyes! Don't you dare!'

He opened his eyes.

'Very dramatic,' he whispered.

'Story to tell the office Tim. I'm not going to do it for you. Keep your eyes open.'

'And look at your ugly face?'

'Yep, and you'll have to look at it for a long time to come.'

I could hear a siren.

'That's the ambulance. You can do it, Tim.'

'Course I can, just keep my eyes open, just keep my ...'

'Tim!'

His eyes were closing, flickering, his fingers lessening their grip on my arm.

'Tim!' I shouted.

The ambulance officers were at my shoulder thanking me, pushing me gently away.

'Tim!'

They were kneeling beside him, their cases open, knowing what to do, experienced, professional, getting him into the ambulance and telling me where to meet them. Then they were driving away with their siren blaring, leaving me with dozens of people gathered around, but I couldn't hear any of them.

We followed in a cab to the same hospital I had been at a few weeks before. We sat in the waiting room, desperate not to fall sleep, but as the night wore on we just couldn't keep our eyes open any longer.

Chapter Eight

The house was only nine years old, a solid two storey stone building that stood defiantly against the harsh moodiness of the ocean. It was winter and the family had moved upstairs, abandoning the lower rooms to the unbearable cold of the north of Scotland. Inside the fire burned fiercely, fighting back the weather that threatened to overwhelm the inhabitants.

Judith sat uneasily on the end of her bed. Thirteen years old, her fingers twirled her hair into tighter and tighter curls. Her bright blue eyes drifted in and out of focus and tears welled up and slipped quickly down her cheeks onto her woollen coat.

'Judith! It's time to go.'

It was her father, a short stout man who had long since lost his hair, but not the laughter that was quick to rise from deep within his belly and intoxicate any room.

Judith heard the words but refused to acknowledge them. She couldn't admit everything was going to change, that this was the end of her life here.

The door opened very slightly.

'Who's there?'

There was a slight movement.

'Daddy?'

Very slowly a nose appeared around the edge of the door.

'Daddy!'

'No, it's not.'

'Yes it is.'

'No, it's not.'

Judith leapt off the bed, raced to the door and grabbed the nose. Immediately her father bundled her into his arms and gave her a dozen kisses.

'I knew it was you!'

'And you were right, my little beauty. Now we must go through to the rest of the family.'

Judith let herself be lowered to the floor and her father led her gently to the room where everyone was fully dressed, ready to leave.

They were sombre, a mixture of fortitude and despair, the atmosphere instantly oppressing the girl. The enormity of what was about to happen burst upon her once again. A lump seized her throat, forcing her to gulp. She had to escape but her two sisters, three brothers, parents, grandparents, and several aunts and uncles stood close, hemming her in, stealing her air. She pushed against them but they didn't move. She became more desperate, finding it harder and harder to breathe until she screamed and barged her way past their surprised looks. She raced down the stairs, wrenched open the front door and stumbled into the garden.

There before her was the ocean, fierce, intimidating, and yet everything that held Judith's small world together. It was her friend, it knew her like no other, its power ran strongly through her blood. Revived, she ran towards it, yearning to be immersed in its understanding.

That day the ocean was in a thunderous mood. The waves raised themselves in anger against the sea wall, demanding to wreak destruction upon the fishing boats huddled together, their masts swinging about in the wind as the froth from the crashing waves leapt onto the wind and hurtled inland.

Judith stood on the dunes, her curls flying in the wind, the cruel freezing blasts ripping through her woollen jacket. The salt water mingled with the tears that streamed down her cheeks.

'I don't want to leave you,' she yelled.

The sea crashed on, pounding against the sand, disregarding her pleas for understanding.

'Please help me, please, please, please.'

She collapsed to her knees, her ears filled with the roar of the ocean.

'Judith.'

It was her father kneeling beside her. She opened her eyes, recognising his love but unable to control herself.

'No!' she screamed, hysterically. 'Don't take me away! Don't take me away!'

She pounded against his chest as he held her, avoiding her eyes, looking out to the horizon, until Judith's anger subsided and she looked up at him. There she saw a painful mixture of love and fear, but there was something more, the same yearning for the ocean that she had within her.

This too was his life, his love, it was what his existence was founded upon, out there on the waves and the clear air. That was his fishing boat in the harbour, the men who worked for him lived in the village. This was his world, even more than Judith's. He was giving this up, abandoning it, casting it away as if it had never existed.

'Why Daddy, why?'

His eyes couldn't leave the mystery of the deepness of the waves as he answered his daughter.

'For my children, for my wife.'

'We could stay.'

'No, times are too tough now, there is nothing we can do. Nothing ...'

'Daddy...'

'No Judith, no. There is nothing more to say. We must fill our hearts with memories of our home, of this ocean, of our place in the world, and then we must go and find a new world where there is still hope.'

Judith was silenced by the look in his eyes, not his words. She couldn't help but trust him, to squeeze his hand as he took hers, to find solidity in him as they faced the ocean together, saying their silent farewells, trying to find hope amidst the pain of leaving their home. Then they turned together and walked back to their waiting family.

Chapter Nine

I was woken from my dream by the surgeon who assured us Tim was going to be all right. I thanked him and stood slowly, looking out the window at London. The city I loved, that loved me, that inspired me, but there was too much going on. Perhaps it was time to get away, maybe I should go up to Scotland, see the old folks, lie low for a while. Eat loads of cakes and wholesome dinners and spend hours talking about the old days and the fishing boats.

Tim looked awful, but he managed a smile.

'I look awful.'

'Yes, you do.'

'Apparently I'm in good shape, which is good news as I haven't written my eulogy yet.'

'And won't for a long while.'

'Unless I take on some more thugs.'

'Don't ever do that again!' exclaimed Jenny.

'Any near death experience?' I asked.

'Dear me no, didn't see any bright light, no one beckoned me into the kingdom. Mind you, no one beckoned me into the darkness, so perhaps I'm not particularly wanted by either side.'

'If there were a side.'

'Ah, now, Charles, being a student of art, you know there's a difference between light and dark, without which we would merely have gray, and that is very dull.'

'Like the food?'

'Just like the food. A poor effort.'

Tim laughed and immediately grimaced.

'I'm not supposed to talk with these stitches, recuperation, rest, that's the story.'

'I'd better leave you to it.'

'I'll be out of here al pronto and then we'll celebrate my recovery.'

'I'll see you soon.'

Tim lay back exhausted by my short visit. I left Jenny with him and went to work. I had a dismally boring time and decided to book tickets to Inverness the next day.

I hired a car at the airport and drove into the Scottish countryside. It was warm, the sky had only a smattering of clouds. I wound down the windows and let the wind blast in. I turned up the music and felt like I'd been on holiday for weeks.

John was in his garden. Short, mid sixties, he had worked all his life in Social Services in Aberdeen and had just moved from their apartment in the city to return to his home.

'John!'

'Charles!'

We shook hands. He was so Scottish, so inwardly warm with a wonderful sense of humour.

'Maureen!'

His wife peered out from the kitchen window, then quickly joined us.

'Charles, how lovely to see you.'

'Lovely to see you too, Maureen.'

'Come in, come in, would you like a cup of tea?'

'Yes please.'

I followed her in, the house so warm and inviting.

'You're in luck, Jack and Kath have been visiting but they left a couple of days ago so you can sleep in the spare bedroom.'

'How long are you up for?' asked Maureen, putting on the kettle.

'Just a day or two.'

'Escape the city and get a bit of fresh sea air?' asked John, lowering himself into an armchair and waving me towards the sofa.

'That sort of thing,' I agreed, sitting, smiling.

It didn't matter how much I loved London, there was no escaping it, this is where my heart lay, where my spirit was at peace. There were no pretences, no need to make excuses or pretend things were different than they were, everyone was family, they all belonged. New members to the family were instantly accepted and introduced to a way of life where the simple things were of greater importance than anything you could purchase. These were honest, wonderful people. Not in any way less intelligent than those who lived in the city, they were very bright, wonderful to talk with late into the night, they just had different priorities, the well-being of a person was foremost.

The weather, the sea, the beauty of the land and the history of their families held them together. Far flung relatives came from all over the world to spend time, to share their stories, to briefly become at one with their history. This was my world, a people and a place of which I was fiercely proud. My family were the most wonderful people who dwelt where the land met the sea.

Maureen appeared with the tea.

'Still no sugar?' she asked.

Always a smile. It was a source of much bemusement that their nephew didn't have sugar with his tea. Very healthy they would say, but I knew they were smiling and acknowledging my city ways.

'I've just done some baking.'

Cookies, smelling like only home made cookies can smell.

'Thank you,' I said, genuinely, knowing I would eat the first one too quickly and be reaching for another before they had finished. There was no stopping myself, they were just so delicious!

'All well?' asked John.

'Tim got stabbed last night.'

'Oh my!' said Maureen. 'Is he all right?'

'He's fine. Decided he wasn't going to give away his money to three guys.'

I told the story, leaving out the part about Tim drinking too much. They were staunch churchgoers and there wasn't much point sullying Tim's good name.

We finished tea and Maureen set to making lunch while John and I made an inspection of the garden.

That evening I went for a walk by myself down to the beach where the ocean crashed against the shore. The waves were building up out past the harbour, drawn inexorably towards the land, in the same way my family had been drawn for generations out into the sea. I stood, mesmerised, counting the seventh wave, trying to prove my granny's theory right that the seventh wave was stronger than the others. It often was but just as often it wasn't. I didn't care, I would always believe it.

She had sat me down on the stony ocean beach in Timaru, New Zealand, where I had spent my childhood, and explained the mysteries of the sea. She had been the first one of the family to leave this village when times were tough in the 1920's, setting off to find a new life with her father on the other side of the world. Leaving behind her mother and the rest of the family to establish a house at the age of 13 for her mother and her brother and sisters to live in when they arrived two years later. That was where I was born, in a town in the South Island of New Zealand, with its small world views and the most beautiful scenery in the world.

My grandfather had taught me how to fish, down on the wharves to start with, then out on his boat when I got older. I can remember the smell of the wharves when I was three, the seagulls, the red cod we hauled up onto the wooden planks. My grandfather's smile, his infectious laughter as he showed his friends the first fish his grandson had caught. I had thought that was the happiest day of my life. But it wasn't, as I got older I had even happier days travelling with my grandfather inland to the rivers with their sweeping currents, fly fishing, listening to his stories from back home, sitting on the stones and eating the lunch my mother had made.

I waved to him and my family at the airport as I caught the plane to fly to Auckland to study at university. That was the last time I saw him. He died of a heart attack on a friend's yacht a month later. I can't really remember the funeral, he was my best friend.

I decided then I would travel to Scotland and meet my

relations, discover the land that had created such extraordinary people. I boarded the plane the day after my final exams. I had no plan, very little money, but I was determined to make my grandparents proud.

The sun was setting with pale red shafts of light painted across the sky. I lay back, the stars gradually appearing, filling the sky with their far away light that seemed so close, so intimate. This was my home, the ocean, the sky, the people, the land that breathed our histories.

I returned to the house to find the others already asleep.

Chapter Ten

Judith woke early that morning, struggling to open her eyes, squinting against the shafts of dazzling sunlight.

'Judith...'

'Mother?'

'Get up quickly dear, it's a beautiful day.'

Judith struggled to move her aged body, willing the meagre life that lingered within her tired muscles to help her out of bed. She hobbled to the front door, opened it, and gasped. She was back in Hopeman. It was the highest tide she'd ever seen, the crashing waves surging right up to the dunes. Her father's fishing boat bobbed about in the harbour where seagulls swooped and dived, screeching above the pounding of the ocean. He was waving and calling to her from the deck.

Suddenly she was joined by dozens of children, laughing and shouting and playing. There was her brother and sisters and friends from school, their eyes bright with the joy of youth. They joined hands and swung her round in giddying circles until they tumbled over the dunes. Then she found herself back in her house in Timaru, her mind still whirling.

Judith dressed and headed off to the local shop. She bought a paper, fumbling for the right coins in her black leather purse, and edged slowly back up the wide road she had walked for the past seventy years. At every step there were memories of people she had loved and lost, all of whom she had outlived. They were there, leaning over their gates, calling out a greeting, offering hands of welcome. Judith's eyes filled with tears.

'This is my home,' she whispered. 'I don't want to leave yet.'

She turned into Seddon Street where old McKenzie crossed the road to greet her. He was holding a bag full of beans.

'Don't worry, Judith,' he smiled. 'The gardening's great.'

'But there's still so much to be done here.'

He shook his head in disbelief.

'Look around you.'

Judith turned slowly, sensing life ebbing away, her limbs struggling to respond. There were people walking towards her, young and old, so many familiar faces, all of them with hands outstretched, smiling, greeting Judith, thanking her for being a part of their lives.

'This is your legacy, Judith. This is your life,' said McKenzie.

Then she was alone again.

Judith pushed open the gate that gently squeaked as it had done for as long as she could remember. She smiled, fingering the roses that had opened to the crispness of the morning light.

She bent down, her face creasing with pain as her long fingers, the skin sagging upon the bone, plucked an offending weed from the garden. It took a long time for her to rise and shuffle through the front door to the kitchen where she made herself a cup of tea.

Judith sat in the lounge, her hands shaking as she raised the cup, the tea spilling into the saucer. She took a sip, then glanced at the paper. War was looming.

'Please Lord, let there be peace. There's been too much war in my lifetime.'

She paused. Her mother was standing in the doorway, smiling.

'It's time dear.'

'Yes, yes it is.'

Judith put the tea down, arranged her skirt and folded her hands in her lap. She slowly looked around the room, at the photographs of her children and grandchildren that filled the ledges, their smiles calming her with warmth and love.

'Thank you,' she whispered, and closed her eyes.

Chapter Eleven

I woke, the dream still inside me, as though my granny had been there in my room. I opened the window and took a deep breath of sea air.

At breakfast there was bacon, tomato, eggs and baked beans. They knew I loved a fry up.

'Tell me, John,' I said, sitting back feeling well overfed. 'What was it like working with poor people?'

John laughed.

'You make it sound like you've never met a poor person.'

'I haven't.'

'Really?'

'Not a really poor person, not like one on the street.'

'Well,' he smiled. 'It's tough in some regards, but on the other hand very rewarding. Poor people are the salt of the earth.'

'I thought you were.'

They laughed.

'I dreamt about granny last night.'

'She was a wonderful woman. She did a lot of good for other people.'

'Yes,' I nodded. 'But I don't.'

'And why not?'

I shrugged. I didn't have an answer.

'I feel like I'm missing out on something, like there's something that I should understand but I don't know what it is. I saw a girl who was helping the poor killed the other day. I saw her, right there, and in her eyes it was like she understood, that she knew what death meant, and so many people knew her, loved her. Hundreds, literally hundreds of people stopped what they were doing and went to the church where they had laid her. But I live there, I work there, and I didn't know her or her world. I was an outsider. There's a whole other world I know nothing about.'

'Then perhaps it's time you discovered their world.'

'How?'

'That's really up to you. Some people work for the poor, some become poor, many ignore them. It's your choice.'

'Become poor?'

'Depends on how much this means to you.'

'I'd have to give up my job.'

'For a while.'

'That's crazy.'

'As I say, it depends on how much it means to you. It sounds like it could mean quite a lot.'

'Still sounds crazy.'

'Some of the most wonderful things in this world are crazy.'

'Perhaps they are,' I smiled, not at all convinced, but the thoughts were whirling round in my mind. I could feel them starting to take form.

Driving back to Inverness, I detoured to the cemetery at Duffus. There was a single church with a tall steeple in the middle of fields where generations of my family were buried. I got out of the car, wandered around and read the inscriptions, some tributes to their lives, others wishing them peace. It wasn't easy even now living in the north of

Scotland with its chilling, bleak winter. To bury someone here in the middle of winter would be a harrowing experience, there was no shelter from the power of the elements. To mourn someone as the cold sweeps through your bones must be an awful thing. Here the spirits of the deceased were laid to rest, no longer battling the sea and the weather, but gone to heaven according to their staunch faith.

These were genuine people, no pretence, no pride in anything except their ability to survive and provide for each other. They were all friends and family, they worked and spent their time together, their world was too small to not know everyone else, the intimate details of their lives, to share their triumphs and their failures. They were a tiny community on the edge of the world and at the end they were all laid together, sharing the same soil, the same mourners.

I was family. They welcomed me, never made me feel like an outsider, but this wasn't my world. My world was in London, working, playing, being with friends. It was a completely different world, something that had satisfied me until the last couple of weeks.

Now I wanted to experience more of life. Standing there in the cemetery I knew I had to discover something more, something else, something I hadn't even thought of before. The poor were the salt of the earth. The girl knew that, my uncle knew that, and now it was time for me to find out what that meant. I was filled with anticipation on the flight home.

Chapter Twelve

I visited Tim at the hospital that night.

'They're letting me go tomorrow.'

'That seems soon.'

'They say I'm a model patient. Marvellous physical condition.'

'You've been hallucinating.'

'Morphine, a strange mix, good for the pain, not so good for the mind. I like to feel awake, in touch, got to get out of here, get back to work, enjoy myself.'

'I'm going to take some annual leave.'

'What on earth for, are you going away?'

'I'm going to become poor.'

'I must still be hallucinating.'

'Something I've never done.'

'Something one should never do.'

'I'll keep you up to date with my progress.'

'Any particular reason for this preposterous decision?'

'Not exactly.'

'Well as long as you haven't thought it through. Do you know exactly how poor you're going to be?'

'Very.'

'Like give up all your possessions?'

'Possibly.'

'And live on the street?'

'I think so.'

'I'm a bit confused, Charles. You haven't had a near death

experience have you? Isn't it me who's supposed to be doing something crazy after being stabbed?'

'Yes you are.'

'Well I'm not. I'm going home to relax for a couple of days, then I'm going back to work.'

'I'll give you a call.'

'How?'

'What?'

'How will you give me a call, you won't have a phone. People on the street don't have mobiles.'

'Then I'll drop by work.'

'You'll stink.'

'Why?'

'You haven't thought about this at all, have you? Nowhere to live means no shower, no clothes, no nothing. You'll be a stinking, unshaven mess. I'll have to meet you in the park.'

'Then I'll meet you in the park.'

'In the park it is, although I have to obviously advise you against this, it is an absurd idea.'

'We shall see.'

'Yes we shall.'

I laughed and waved goodbye as I left. But truth be known, I really didn't know what I was going to do, or how, or even where to start, or, more seriously, how far I was planning to go, where I was going to end up. Perhaps it was just crazy.

Chapter Thirteen

Day 1 of being poor. When I woke up I had completely forgotten about my plans. It wasn't until I was eating a grapefruit as the coffee gurgled in the machine that I remembered this was my first day of poverty.

So time for a plan. I reached for a pen and a piece of paper. First things first, how serious was I going to be? There's being poor and then there's being really poor. And what sort of safety net was I going to put in place? Do I keep the house? Of course I keep the house. But do I keep living in the house? Well that didn't make sense. I had to move out. So how many clothes/possessions could I take with me? A bag, a big bag, a small bag? And could I access money, and if so, how much?

I had to have a coffee. It might be my last coffee. Poor people can't afford delicious coffee, get what I'm given, but who will give me anything? Was I going to queue with the Salvation Army or the Hari Krishnas? I had seen them with a sort of mobile kitchen, that could be healthy but how often do they do it? And where was I going to sleep? In a hostel? That sounded pretty awful, dozens of smelly men. Probably best to find a nice little bench somewhere, as long as it was fine, of course.

But how long was I doing this for, a week, a couple of weeks, a month? A month might be about right, but it seemed a long time to sleep on a park bench. And what was I doing this for again? Something to do with finding out about the other side of life I'd never experienced ... but I didn't need to ever experience it ... but then I would always wonder why that girl had seemed so peaceful when she died, why all those people had loved her, whether I could ever be like that.

That was it, wasn't it? I wanted to know if I could ever be like her, do what she did, have that look in my eye, gaze into a *van Gogh* painting and know that I belonged, that I had a valid reason for existing. I wanted to know that my life counted for something, that when I died I wouldn't just be buried in the ground, that people would be genuinely sorry I was gone, that they would respect me for what I had done, for who I was.

So what did I need? It was Summer so that was a bonus. I would definitely only use a backpack, just a small one, so I gathered up some clothes, toothpaste, that sort of thing. And money, I still wasn't sure about that. I didn't want to starve. Perhaps £100, no that seemed too much. £50? Seemed ridiculous, wouldn't manage a decent night out for £50. But this was about having no money. So I finished packing, locked the door and headed off.

And now what? I didn't have a clue. What do poor people do? How do they fill in their days if they're not working? I headed towards the hostel on Arlington Road thinking that I could get some clues if I hung around there.

So I did, for a couple of hours. Ten o'clock in the morning and the men in their old ripped suits drifted in and out of the hostel, mostly by themselves, occasionally with a mate. Some of them were talking loudly, some of them arguing, some of them were carrying beer cans, the preference being either Guinness or Fosters. I followed a couple of them wanting to see where they went, what they did, how they filled in the hours. They shuffled down to the off-licence, bought a couple of cans each, sat on the wooden bench and drank and discussed football. Then they returned to the hostel, helping each other along the road, swaying more than when they left.

There were a multitude of workers going in and out of the hostel, some of them carrying what I presumed were drugs in their locked kits. They greeted the people who lived there by name, stopping to discuss things with them, cheerfully shaking hands or giving them a slap on the back as they carried on their work.

Certainly no revelation yet. It seemed a little sad these old men trundling around, some of them yelling at imaginary figures. Time for lunch. Ah, now, here was my first decision. I had £50, so lunch would have to be cheap, really cheap. So cafés, restaurants and pubs were all out of the question. I had to find a sandwich. Marks and Spencer's, I knew they had sandwiches. I wandered in, feeling like I had solved my first problem, but as I looked at their array it struck me the people selecting their sandwiches were well dressed. This was not where the poor came for lunch. So where else? Another supermarket, Prêt a Porter, a corner shop? It was time to research. And what to eat? Sandwiches seemed the logical solution but perhaps that was presumptuous. What about other types of food, like hot chips, they were filling and cheap. But if I got them I'd have to get something like an apple. I couldn't just fill myself with carbohydrates, that wasn't going to work.

I smiled. There were a lot of things to work out, this was more complicated than fasting.

I settled for chips and wandered up to the park. Another gorgeous day. I found my spot and ate the chips, enjoying their saltiness. I lay back in the sun and let myself drift off to sleep.

Chapter Fourteen

Stephanie was a beautiful little girl. She was very kind and full of love. But she was unhappy. Her mother had just died and she thought that maybe her mother had died because she had been a bad girl.

Stephanie lay in a field in the middle of the countryside with hundreds of differently coloured flowers about her.

In the bright blue sky were little puffy clouds that formed the shapes of animals. They darted about, stopping here and there to talk with other clouds.

Above the clouds was the Sun who had a huge smile on his face. He talked to the clouds as they scuttled past. Every so often one of the clouds would make the Sun laugh and warm rays would fly off him.

As Stephanie lay there on the ground looking up at the clouds, an owl flew down and perched on a branch in the tree above her. It was a large owl with big brown round eyes and it looked very wise.

'Hello owl,' Stephanie said.

'Hello Stephanie,' replied the owl.

'How do you know my name?' asked Stephanie.

'I am very wise,' said the owl.

'Then do you know the answer to everything?' asked Stephanie.

'Almost everything,' replied the owl. 'What would you like to know?'

Stephanie thought for a long time. Finally she asked, 'Can

you tell me if I am a good or a bad little girl?'

The owl blinked. It raised its head and said that she would only find the answer to that question if she flew to the Moon.

'But the Moon is so far away!' exclaimed Stephanie.

'Not as far as you think,' replied the wise owl, fluttering his wings, ready to fly off.

'Don't go,' said Stephanie. 'You have to tell me how to get to the Moon.'

'You will find a way,' said the owl wisely.

Then he flew off his perch into the sky where, with a few beats of his wings, he disappeared.

Stephanie looked up to the Sun in the sky. She knew that behind it was the Moon, but there seemed no way to reach it. Tears came to her eyes and trickled down her cheeks.

The clouds saw her tears and flitted down to look at the beautiful girl on the grass. They talked quickly to each other, amazed that such a pretty young thing could feel so sad.

They darted about and played games and told stories but nothing caught her attention. She was filled with misery because she didn't know how to get to the Moon.

Finally one of the youngest clouds daringly came close and floated in front of Stephanie.

'What's wrong?' she asked.

Stephanie looked up and saw the bluest eyes she'd ever seen. They were light and fresh and full of the joy of life.

'I want to go to the Moon,' she said.

The cloud smiled at her.

'Why are you smiling?' asked Stephanie.

'What you are wanting to do is the easiest thing in the world,' said the cloud. 'All you have to do is ask.'

'Ask who?'

'Ask me,' laughed the cloud.

Was it possible that this tiny delicate thing could take her to the Moon?

Stephanie thought of the distance and travelling through the atmosphere and the lack of oxygen and she realised that it was impossible. She sank back into the grass, resting her head in her hands.

'All you have to do is ask,' said the cloud again. 'If you do I'll take you to the Moon.'

Stephanie knew it wasn't possible. But she decided to ask anyway, there seemed to be no harm in doing that.

The cloud was so happy Stephanie had asked it to take her to the moon that it leapt into the air and darted all around her. It laughed and talked and sang songs all at once.

Then it hovered above the ground in front of Stephanie and she got onto it and in an instant they were soaring upwards.

The air grew cold as they flew amongst the other clouds that said hello. Some were old and some were young. Stephanie said hello to several of them and found out where they had come from.

Then they flew above them and went into space where everything changed and became colder and darker. Stephanie looked back at the beauty of her hair trailing behind her as if she were a comet, breaking into millions of different coloured sparks that formed a trail back to the earth.

Then the cloud headed straight for the Sun, a huge ball of fire in space.

Stephanie screamed. She thought she was going to die. Her scream was drowned out by the loud noise of the rivers of fire that flowed about the surface of the Sun.

The cloud flew down and landed on one of the rivers. Then they were whirling around the Sun on the waves of fire. Out of the river flew tiny sparks of light that rose up and then burst like tiny fireworks.

'Take a drink,' said the cloud.

'Of the river?' asked Stephanie.

'Reach over and scoop it up in your hands.'

Stephanie bent down and touched the fire which sparked and exploded all around her. She took some in her hands and felt her skin tingle as she drank it. It wasn't like liquid, it was air filled with millions of tiny bubbles all popping and tingling within her.

She laughed and the sunlight filled her lungs with joy. It was the first time she had felt happy for a long time.

She drank some more and started to dance and sing until they reached the other side of the Sun.

The Moon appeared before them. It was cold and gray and covered in deep dark seas.

The cloud lifted off the wave and started to fly towards it.

'Don't go,' cried Stephanie. 'Let's stay here.'

'But you will never discover who you are,' said the cloud.

'This is all I want to be.'

'But this is the Sun. You've got to go to the Moon to find out who you are.'

Stephanie looked again at the dark and imposing figure of the Moon and was filled with fear. If that was where she had to go to discover if she was good or bad, then it could only mean bad news. If she stayed on the Sun she would always be filled with light.

'I'm going to stay here.'

'But you will die,' said the cloud, who was getting very worried. 'Anyone who stays on the Sun dies after one hour.'

Stephanie felt the warmth and fun of the light popping within her. She couldn't believe that it could kill her.

'I'm staying,' she said.

'Then I shall have to leave you,' said the cloud.

'But we're having such fun.'

'I don't want to die,' said the cloud, slowing as much as she could to let Stephanie get off.

Stephanie stood on the edge of the cloud and looked about her at the beauty of the Sun. She took a step out onto it. But as she did so the river rose up around her, as if it wanted to attack her. She took her foot back in and the river smoothed again.

'It will kill you,' said the cloud. 'It won't let anything live here unless it is pure light.'

Stephanie stepped out again and the river rose up to meet her, snarling, its flames licking at her feet.

'But why must I go there?' she demanded, pointing at the Moon.

'Because you must.'

'I don't want to.'

'No one does until they get there and we've come so far we may as well go on,' said the cloud, hopefully.

Stephanie sat down again. What had seemed a wonderful adventure had turned into a nightmare. She was surrounded by fire that wanted to destroy her and a Moon that was dark and cold.

The cloud headed for the Moon. Stephanie sat silently, waiting for something terrible to happen.

As the Moon came closer it became colder and darker. Everything was gray and dead. Stephanie wrapped her arms about herself to keep warm as they drew near.

Then they landed. Alone. There was no life there. Just a vast wilderness of mountains and craters.

She stepped off the cloud and walked a few steps, finding the ground painful on her feet after the lightness of the cloud. All about her was a feeling of nothingness. The air was painful in her chest, the stars in the sky seemed far far away.

Stephanie was afraid. She turned around to ask the cloud to take her back home. But it was gone!

She had been abandoned! She started to run, trying to escape, bruising her feet against the hard rocks. On and on and on she ran until her legs collapsed under her and she fell to the ground.

In front of her was some water. Just a few feet away. She tried to drag herself along the ground to reach it but the rocks cut her legs. So she used all of her strength to stand up and she walked very painfully to the water.

Then Stephanie saw a light in the water. At first it was very faint, but as she looked it grew brighter and brighter and started to form the shape of a person.

She looked harder, trying to discover who it was. It moved slightly as she did, looking up to her as she looked down. Then Stephanie saw that it was her. A reflection of herself.

The reflection grew brighter and brighter until she could see herself clearly.

Stephanie saw that she was incredibly beautiful. Her eyes shone like the Sun, her hair was long and shining.

Then more images started to appear in the water. The green grass and trees and the sky and Sun appeared and she was amazed at the beauty and wonder of everything she saw. It had never seemed like this on the real earth.

Stephanie suddenly found herself back in the field at home. The clouds were still playing and the Sun was smiling. But as she looked about her, Stephanie saw that the world she had seen in the reflection on the Moon was still around her, it was just the same.

The countryside was filled with life and colour. She spread her arms wide and felt the goodness of the world within her.

I woke up and a girl was sitting beside me.

'It's strange being on a journey when you don't know where you're heading,' she said.

'Yes it is,' I replied, not quite conscious, not quite sure why a girl was talking to me.

'But exciting.'

'Exciting,' I agreed, regaining consciousness.

She smiled.

'How was the goldfish?'

'A marvel.'

'I knew it would be.'

'You know quite a lot.'

'I like to find out people's stories. But I never know the

endings. I know the possibilities but I never know the last scene, there are so many choices. That's what intrigues me.'

'So you don't know what will happen to me when the curtain falls?'

'Why should I? Life is always more fun when you don't know how the day is going to pan out.'

'Recommendations?'

'None at all. Why spoil your fun?'

She smiled and stood, picking up her bicycle off the grass.

'Time to go.'

'I'll see you again?'

'More than likely. Enjoy the sunshine!'

I watched her go, strangely peaceful. I had just had what many would call a delusional moment with a beautiful girl who was probably an angel of some description. She didn't disappear in a puff of smoke which was a little disappointing, she just rode away over the rolling fields, her hair flying in the gentle breeze.

Now I was poor but I had met an angel. I wanted to talk about it with someone, but everyone I knew would agree that I had lost my marbles. So I headed for the canal, my naked friends would enjoy my tall tales.

Chapter Fifteen

Andrew and Jess weren't naked, or having breakfast, they were just sitting normally at the back of the houseboat reading the morning newspaper.

'Hi guys.'

'Charles!'

They leapt up to give me a hug as though I were one of their closest friends.

'Haven't seen your friend for ages.'

'No, they're talking now.'

'That's fantastic.'

'And you?' asked Jess, smiling.

'I've become poor.'

'Really? By choice?'

'I have decided to be poor.'

'Then you'll be just like us,' laughed Andrew.

'You're not poor!'

'Of course we are. Why do you think we live on a houseboat?'

'I thought you were a little crazy.'

'Well, yeah, sure, but we also have got very little money so this is our home.'

'It never occurred to me.'

'Probably because you've never been poor.'

'True. I know nothing about it.'

'Do you want some tips?' asked Jess.

'That would be really helpful.'

'How many days have you been poor?'

'This is the first one.'

'Caught you early.'

'I just don't know what poor people do.'

'A lot more than you'd think. Would you like a drink?' asked Jess.

I hesitated, now knowing that they didn't have much, thinking about the amount of bacon I'd eaten last time, how much that would have cost them.

'Okay, rule number one, Charles, if someone offers you anything you always, and I mean always, accept it. Without exception.'

'Then yes, sorry, yes please.'

Andrew poured some orange juice.

'Now we'll show you what we do.'

We left the houseboat and wandered down the canal, Jess carrying a bag.

Every so often they stopped and picked flowers. After a while we came to a dinghy tied up under a bridge.

'This is the local dinghy we all use. Take it, use it, return it. Feel free to borrow it whenever you want.'

Andrew rowed along the far shore. We stopped at several of the houses whose lawns backed onto the canal. The owners waved and some of them came down and welcomed us, discussing the day and tidbits of their lives as they helped us gather flowers from their gardens.

'You've got a new friend,' called a woman from her garden as we approached. 'You must have lunch and introduce me.'

Emma had the food laid out on her bench.

'Do grab a plate. I thought we could sit on the patio.'

We sat down and started to eat, discussing the weather and the state of the canal.

'So Charles, tell me, what do you do?'

'Well, I've just given up my job and am going to live on park benches.'

'Oh marvellous! And what are you going to do?'

'I'm not sure.'

'But you'll have so much time on your hands. You can do anything you want! The world is your oyster!'

'I hadn't thought of it that way.'

'But you must, and you must keep me up to date, drop by and have lunch, afternoon tea, whenever you feel like it. It's wonderful news. Your life has become a blank canvas.'

She leapt to her feet.

'I've got something to show you.'

She dashed away and hurried back holding a painting.

'Here's my latest work, do you love it?'

'Of course we love it!' exclaimed Jess.

'I've got my auction tonight. You are all coming aren't you?'

'We'll be there,' said Andrew.

'Marvellous!'

After lunch we rowed back to the bridge laden down with flowers which we took to the houseboat. For the next couple of hours I sat mesmerised as they exchanged the dried flowers around the houseboat for the new flowers. They created the most extraordinary designs with the dried flowers. I've never had any interest in flower design but I was amazed by the colours, the different textures, the coloured twine, the precision with which they mixed and mingled. They really were works of art.

'Can you give us a hand to take them?'

'Sure,' I agreed, carefully holding a basket.

We walked through the traffic to a two storied semi-detached house.

Andrew opened the door.

'We just go on through.'

There was a dark corridor with a single naked bulb hanging from the ceiling. We carefully climbed the stairs, creaking, old Turner reproduction paintings on the wall. Then Andrew opened the door and we were momentarily blinded by the sunshine.

It was a room with the old cream paint peeling, some if it hanging off the walls. The windows were large but dirty and smeared on the outside making the view unfocused. There was a combination of posters and cheaply framed prints around the room. And eight beds.

They were old hospital beds, steel, covered in blankets. In the beds sat eight elderly ladies. Some wore crudely applied makeup, others no makeup at all. All of them had spots and blotches on their faces, their hands lying on top of the blankets, thin and wrinkled.

'Good afternoon girls!' called out Andrew.

They turned as one, recognised the couple and broke into smiles and laughter, clapping their hands and gesturing in welcome. Andrew and Jess moved quickly from one to another giving them hugs and kisses and handed each of them bunches of flowers.

The old women were overwhelmed by their beauty and

held them up to the sunlight, twirling them round and round, a couple of them fixing them to their tops.

'Now I'd like you all to meet Charles, a new friend. He'll be coming here for the next few weeks.'

They introduced themselves, where they came from, how long they had been there. The remarkable thing was they had all been fashion models years before.

'And what do you do, young man?' asked Beth.

'I did work for a publishing firm, but ...'

I couldn't get any further, they were so interested. They asked me all sorts of questions, where I came from, at what university I'd studied, who I knew, what artists I had met, where my family was, where I lived.

'I'm homeless at the moment.'

'You can always stay here,' laughed Hilda.

'Hilda!' said Maggie sternly.

'I could do with a young man around.'

'I'm sure you could, but you know the rules. No boyfriends in the house.'

'Now who made that rule?' asked Ruth.

'We all agreed on the rules.'

'But that was so long ago,' exclaimed Hilda. 'Sometimes I think we were a little strict on ourselves.'

'We could vote,' offered Diane.

'That's a good idea!'

I looked around the room and considered staying with these eight old dears.

'I'm sure I'd be a nuisance.'

'Not at all!'

'I've got all sorts of annoying little habits. You'd soon

grow tired of me.'

'Men are a trifle annoying,' said Hilda. 'I know Johnnie could drive me round the bend.'

'Jack would never put his paper back in the basket.'

'And Norm, my, he could snore!'

'Do you snore?'

'Apparently.'

'Loudly?'

'I have been known to snore loudly.'

'That wouldn't be so good,' acknowledged Hilda, sadly.

'But I could get you some books.'

'That you publish?'

'What would you like?'

Well that started them off. They had a lady who dropped by with magazines, but they didn't get many books so I agreed to bring back as many as I could carry the next day.

'And now we'd better be going. It's Emma's auction tonight.'

'Oh, tonight, already? My how time flies,' said Judith. 'I hope it's a wonderful success.'

'Send her our love.'

'I certainly will. We'll be back next week.'

'Don't forget the books Charles, it will be wonderful to have some new things to read.'

We waved goodbye and headed back downstairs.

We visited three more houses where old ladies lived together, all of them so friendly and welcoming. I had to tell my story again and agreed to take books to all of them. It was early evening when we had given away all the flowers.

Chapter Sixteen

We arrived at the auction at 7.30pm. It was upstairs in a brick building near the lock, nowhere I'd been before but I had a feeling I was going to discover lots of new places. It was large with wooden floors, white walls, but hard to describe more than that because it was jam packed with people, and I mean people in the broadest sense of the word. Men and women in beautifully cut suits, others in expensive casual jeans and tops, a great deal of what I presumed were students, and poor people. Their clothes were old, the suits were rumpled, the skirts ripped. It was a snapshot of London's ethnic diversity all talking with each other, with tons of smiles, laughter and stories being shared.

Drinks were off to one side and in the middle were several tables stacked with food. Everyone had something in their hand. Youngsters rushed with trays to restock the table and to serve platters to the assembled throng.

We started towards the drinks table when Emma came dashing over to meet us.

'Darlings!' she exclaimed. 'Sooo lovely of you to come. Do have a drink. Louise, drinks please, thank you dear. Isn't it marvellous? All my friends have come, we're going to have such a fun night.'

And she was off, to be encircled by people wanting to talk with her.

'Charles!'

It was Nigel. He managed a floor of an investment bank.

'Nigel,' I replied, shaking hands.

'Haven't seen you for ages. What are you up to? Still publishing those extravagant tales?'

'I'm on vacation.'

'And yet you're here?'

'Yes ...'

I didn't have a clue how to respond. It seemed ridiculous to say I was being poor, how silly did that sound?

'So which one are you planning to buy?'

'I'm not sure yet.'

'Let me show you round. I can tell you which ones I'm bidding for and we can try and outdo each other.'

'I'm not sure I'll be bidding.'

'Really?'

'Well, I'm sort of ...'

Why couldn't I just come out with it? If it was something I truly believed in then I should be able to talk about it.

'I've decided to be poor.'

'Really? How extraordinary! And is this your decision or has it been cast upon you?'

'No, my decision, I feel a bit foolish talking about it.'

'Charles, what is life but a series of adventures? You'll discover a whole world you never knew existed.'

'I hope so.'

'Then enjoy it. The world is a vast and amazing place. Bet you didn't know this place was here till tonight.'

'No.'

'And yet it's been here for over twenty years. Every six months we have a different artist. Just fantastic! Such a wonderful evening. Have fun.'

And with that he was gone, suddenly disappearing to the other side of the room as a waiter offered me more food.

A youngish guy approached me, perhaps mid twenties, his hair was slick, not with hair product but with not having washed it for some time. He wore a blue suit, pin stripe, the jacket and trousers didn't match, and a white shirt, stained collar and a worn tie. His face was lean. I could see the jaw bone clearly, and two nasty looking spots above his left eye.

'Good evening, my name's Steve.'

'Hi Steve, Charles.'

His hand took mine. There were tattoos on the fingers but I didn't have time to make out what they said.

'I love Emma's art.'

'I haven't been able to see it yet.'

'Then I'll show you, this way.'

I could have just let him disappear into the crowd, it seemed the safest option. My hand felt clammy, there was a dark smear on my palm. But he looked back and gestured for me to follow.

'Aren't they fantastic?'

I nodded my head in reply, realising who this woman was, Emma Cottrell, a hugely successful and admired artistic recluse who never made public appearances.

'Ethereal but without sentimentality, as though heaven and earth are meeting on the surface of the water.'

I looked at this man I had wanted to ignore.

'Are you an artist?'

'Depends on your definition. I work on the Peckham Common estates after midnight.'

'After midnight ...?'

There was the loud ringing of a spoon on glass to bring us to silence. A man who I thought I recognised made his way to the microphone.

'Ladies and Gentlemen, it is my privilege to welcome you here this evening. My name is John Dalloway and I am thrilled to be the patron of these exhibitions and auctions.'

Crikey I thought, serious aristocracy, he owned chunks of London.

'So on behalf of myself and my committee, welcome. And welcome especially to Emma. Your work is wonderful and your generosity exceeds us all.'

There was an eruption of applause.

'Thank you John. You are a light for so many of our young artists. I hope we can raise a little money tonight for such a good cause.'

The auction began and two hours later it was over. £180,000 had been raised. Everyone was ecstatic, there were huge cheers after every picture was sold.

'And now, the reason why we are here,' said John, beaming. 'We have eight artists who are the recipients of this auction. They are all doing absolutely wonderful work in their communities.'

He brought the eight forward, describing where they were working and how they were encouraging teenagers to develop their art.

Emma and John went from one to the other, shaking their hands, talking to them, taking their time while applause rippled around the room.

'What a great night!'

Nigel was at my shoulder.

'You must drop by sometime soon and share some of your stories. I'm really looking forward to it.'

'Will do,' I smiled, watching him leave holding a painting.

'Charles, so good of you to come.'

Emma was positively beaming.

'A privilege.'

'I hear you're a writer.'

'I work for a publisher.'

'Of course you do, but prior to that you wrote some wonderful articles, mainly on new art. Most of it wasn't my cup of tea but I loved reading them.'

'You're going back a few years.'

'Not that many! Now look, how would you like to write for me?'

'I haven't done anything for ages. I could be a bit rusty.'

'It will come back to you. I've lined up *ArtsNow*. I showed them your work and the artists you saw tonight and they're dead keen.'

'I could …'

'Marvellous. No money I'm afraid, my policy with everything I do. They'll donate the fees to the fund for artists in developing countries, is that okay?'

'Sure.'

'Marvellous. I saw you meet Steve, a brilliant young man. Now let me introduce you to the others.'

After a whirlwind tour, Andrew and Jess approached.

'Time to sleep,' declared Jess.

'Absolutely,' I agreed.

Then I realised I didn't have anywhere to sleep. I had been on the go all day and hadn't had time to think about it.

'You can stay with us if you like?' suggested Andrew.

That seemed like an easy option, a roof over my head and friendly people, but of course that wasn't the point. I was trying to discover another world and doing it the easy way wasn't the plan.

'I'd love to but I thought I'd sleep on a park bench or something, you know, first night of my adventure and all.'

'I understand,' smiled Andrew. 'Sleep rough, see how painful it really is. Have you lined up somewhere?'

'Not yet.'

'Then why don't you try the bench beside the house boat? That way you can sleep rough but you'll be safe.'

'We've got a couple of spare blankets,' added Jess.

'That would be perfect.'

'There we go! And you've had dinner already.'

'Couldn't ask for more.'

After getting the blankets and a pillow out of the houseboat, I approached the bench slowly. There was a logistical problem. The bench was about five feet long with wooden slats and iron handles at the ends. I was six feet tall. My legs would either have to go over the sides, over the end, or curl up. All the options seemed as uncomfortable as the others so I decided to start with them over the end.

The world is very different when you're lying on a park bench trying to sleep. When you're in bed at home and the lights are turned out it seems that the world is silent. When you're lying on a park bench beside a canal you realise that the world is very much alive. There were dozens of different sounds, the swishing of the water hurrying by, the small animals ferreting in the undergrowth, the odd bird flying past. And fish jumping in the water. Pathetic tiny little fish you wouldn't normally notice that made extraordinarily loud splashing sounds as they belly flopped back into the canal. There was no way in the world I was ever going to sleep. I could even see the reflection of the lights on the water from the moon and the lamplights when I closed my eyes.

So I gave up and lay there enjoying the beauty of the world that was alive with the creatures of the night.

'It's a lovely night, don't you think?'

I started, sitting up quickly.

'No need to worry, it's just old Liam.'

A man sat down next to me, his body shaking as he manoeuvred himself onto the chair and placed his cane against his leg.

'You're new around here.'

'I'm normally here during the day.'

'So what brings you out at night? A chance to gaze at the moon, or perhaps your wife and yourself have had a little altercation?'

'No, there's no wife.'

'A truly fortunate man, not a care in the world.'

'Not a care in the world.'

'Are you perhaps a poet?'

His eyes looked at me intensely, shining with the light off the water. There were wrinkles, but not the wearisome type, they were those caused by laughter, by warm smiles, by friendship. He wore a coat, a very old coat, and a crumpled hat.

'No, but I'm sure you're a poet.'

'Ah, yes, that I be.'

'From Cornwall?'

'And proud of it.'

'So why are you here in London?'

'Is this not the city where the streets are paved with gold?'

'You have come to find your fortune?'

'That I have.'

'And have you found any gold?'

'Not of the type envisaged. But I have certainly found much gold.'

'And where might that be?'

He raised his hand slowly, turned it into a fist and beat it on his chest.

'In here, in my heart, in the hearts of the people. So much gold, they have given me so much gold. I am weighed down with all their riches.'

'So are you returning home?'

'One day soon, one day soon.'

'And how long have you been here?'

'Twenty six years I have walked these streets.'

'A wandering poet.'

'Yes, a wandering poet.'

He leant forward.

'The moon is half full tonight, as is this city, half full of light, and half full of darkness. As are the cities of the world, and where there are the darkest shadows there also is the brightest light. That is why I live in the darkness of the night. It is here I find the most beautiful light.'

I nodded, slowly.

'I sense you have never been overwhelmed by the light?'

'Not overwhelmed, as such.'

'Perhaps you have never been helplessly in love?' he said.

'No.'

'You have never truly lived?'

I didn't respond.

'Your heart has only beaten slowly.'

I wanted to think of something clever, something witty to say, some sort of response that would justify my existence. But nothing came. I had never been completely overwhelmed, never let myself go. I had always been in control, dictating how I wanted situations to unfold. I had admired, been admired, I had charmed, been continually invited to social events where I was the centre of attention. I had enjoyed women, enjoyed their beauty, their smiles, their bodies, but I had never been overwhelmed. I had never been consumed, taken, possessed, been out of control.

'My heart has only beaten slowly.'

'So you are on a quest?'

'Yes, perhaps I am.'

'Then I wish you well. I am a poet. I have drunk from the cup of this city and have poured my soul into its soul. There is nothing I could ever want more than I have now.'

'What do you have now?'

'In your eyes, I have nothing.'

'But in your heart?'

'Dwell the wonders of this world.'

He stood, leaning on his cane.

'My name is Liam Norwood, a poet.'

I stood and extended my hand.

'My name is Charles Latimer, and it has been an honour

to meet you.'

I shook his hand and he passed a piece of paper to me.

'Until we meet again in the light of the darkness.'

He turned and walked away silently into the night.

I sat down and unscrumpled the piece of paper. Barely legible were the scrawlings of an old man.

A Black Dress
It was late, very late, or perhaps early,
a slight glow searching the horizon
as she sat there,
her eyes reflecting the lights on the river,
brows furrowed, back straight,
long fingers toying with a silver cross.
A girl, a woman, a wandering spirit,
the water swirling towards her,
she calling it, it calling her?
At one with each other,
every night, sitting there alone, for one year exactly.
I know because I too have been there, every night,
motionless, at one with her, the water, the night lights,
no longer searching, knowing, silently knowing.
And now a new day, and we both rise, wordless,
returning to the shadows of the light,
yearning for the clear focus of the night.

Chapter Seventeen

I managed to sleep for a couple of hours before I accepted Andrew's early words of welcome and invitation to breakfast. Then with the promise of a warm day I headed off alone.

I walked for about an hour, enjoying watching people rushing to work, the cars, taxis and buses that were packed with people from every country on the planet. London was filled with so many people, so much colour, so many different languages. I began to search for the gold, for the London that Liam Norwood the poet had found. I paused to enjoy the smiles, the little children playing, the old people telling stories, the jokes, the calling out across the streets, the words of love shared on mobile phones as people hurried to their jobs. In the parks people were walking their dogs, parents and children were playing before they went to school. This was the London that was filled with people's hopes and ambitions, the businesses and shops where many immigrants had come to seek their fortune and live a life previously denied them. Even the down and outs were meeting others and sharing a tale or two about what had happened in the night while they were sleeping under the alcove of a church door or under a tree in the park.

I stood on a bridge and watched the trains rumble in, bringing hundreds of people into the city. The sun shone through the leaves, casting their shadows onto the ever brightening cobblestones.

I sat on a bench beside a vendor selling coffee. Dozens of people came up to him, most knowing him by name, saying hello, wishing him a good day. He served their coffee quickly, careful not to spill any, asking them how they were, how work was, what their children were doing. Then a mother and child came up behind him and the child grabbed hold of his leg. He immediately smiled, turned, picked the child up and gave her a huge kiss. She laughed and laughed and he twirled her round. He kissed the woman and gave her a hug. The people standing in queue smiled and said hello to the little girl. Then they were gone and he continued with his work, discussing how his daughter was doing at school. I carried on walking, not caring where I was going.

About ten o'clock I came across a man dressed in a clown suit making balloon animals for a group of youngsters and their mothers. The children were about three, all smiling and laughing, gathering in number by the minute. Their mothers held them by the hand or knelt down at the front with them, enjoying it as much as their children.

The clown twisted and turned the balloons and snapped the legs of the animals into positions. He made lots of funny comments to the children and produced the animals as though they were the most wonderful things he had ever seen.

They were in raptures, begging him to make one for them, shouting out the names of the animals he should make. He handed them over to shouts of glee and they ran to show their mothers.

The clown saw me and stopped for a moment. Then he raised his hand.

'Girls and boys, another clown!'

I looked around to check there wasn't someone behind me.

'A brilliant, fantastic clown, give him a big clap.'

I didn't know what to do. There were a dozen children gazing at me, clapping, their eyes shining with expectation. I couldn't say I wasn't a clown, that would upset them, but I didn't have any acts, anything I could do to entertain them. I had always stayed clear of children if the truth be known. I made up desperate and sometimes not at all true excuses for avoiding birthday parties.

'He's a bit shy because he hasn't got his clown suit on. We'll have to encourage him. Come on boys and girls, come on Charlie, Charlie the Clown, do something for us, come on Charlie!'

They all started yelling 'Come on Charlie,' pleading with me, and their mothers joined in, gesturing with their hands.

I desperately thought what to do, what to do, how did he know my name, who was this, what could I do?

I allowed myself to be led in front of the group, and stood there, smiling, trying to think.

'Tell us a story,' called the clown, now standing with the parents.

'Tell us a story,' they all joined in.

Then all the parts within me that wanted to say no suddenly melted away. I wanted to share something with these children. I could tell they had nothing. Their eyes were bright and shining but their clothes were ripped and old, cheap stuff that was falling apart, and a few of them had nasty looking cuts and sores.

'Tell us a story!' they yelled, imploring, hoping.

'Tell us a story,' added the parents.

I took a deep breath and started, hesitantly at first, as their wide entranced eyes opened my heart a little. As I shared myself with them, they shared their love and joy with me, and it reached inside and made me smile as I sat on the paving stones in the midst of this ragged bunch of children.

'Does anyone know what an albatross is?' I asked.

They shook their heads.

'Does anyone know what a seagull is?'

'It's a bird!' they shouted.

'And what colour is it?'

'White!'

'And what do birds do?'

'They fly!'

'Yes they do. Now an albatross is like a seagull but it is ten times bigger than a seagull. It's as big as from here to that post there.'

'That's huge!' said a little girl.

'Yes it is, and they fly for miles and miles without having to land. Their wings are bigger than you.'

'Bigger than me?' asked a boy, standing up.

'Bigger than you.'

'That's huge!' repeated the little girl.

'Yes it is. And has anyone heard of the Falkland Islands?'

'Nooo,' they shook their heads.

'It's a long long way away, near Antarctica at the bottom of the world. And on their island there was a little boy called Robert who lived with his father and mother. The island could get very cold in the winter because it was near

Antarctica where the polar bears and seals lived. There were gales and the wind drove the waves up against the cliffs of the island sending spray high up into the air. They lived on a farm and they had lots of animals. There were hens that laid eggs and roosters and chickens and pigs and cows and sheep and two black and white sheep dogs called Izzy and Lizzy.

Robert loved to run. When he was very little he couldn't run very fast because his legs were so short. As he grew taller he began to race against the sheep and the cows. He was so fast he was able to beat them and this made him very happy. Then he raced against the sheep dogs. They were too fast for him when he tried the first time. But one day he ran so quickly that he won. He had beaten the sheep dogs!

Now Jemma was an albatross. She lived on the island with her mother and two brothers. Jemma raced them across the sky and because she was the fastest and the strongest she always won. Her wings were so wide and she beat them so quickly no one could keep up with her.

One day Jemma saw Robert running across the field. Jemma flew down beside him. Robert waved and ran faster. Jemma sped up and so did Robert.

Robert's legs went faster and faster until he could hardly see them beneath him. Jemma beat her wings harder and harder, the ground whirring past underneath her.

Then suddenly Robert came to the edge of a cliff. But he was running so fast he couldn't stop and he ran straight over the edge. Beneath him were rocks and the white foam of the waves crashing against the rocks. He could hear them as he fell towards them. Then there was the loud whooshing of wings. Jemma flew down underneath him and picked him up on her back. He was safe!

Jemma flew up high above the land. Robert looked down and saw the island. There was his house made out of red brick and the tractor and the pigs in their pen. He could see the sheep and the cows on the fields but as the albatross flew higher they became little white and brown dots on the green of the grass.

Robert wasn't afraid. He held onto the albatross' neck and looked out to sea where they were heading.

'Thank you very much for saving me,' said Robert.

'That's alright,' said Jemma. 'You are a very fast runner.'

Robert was surprised. He didn't know albatrosses could speak. But they are very special birds. Many sailors lost on the sea have had an albatross come and land on their boat and tell them the way to get home.

'What is your name?' asked Jemma.

'Robert,' he replied.

'My name is Jemma,' said the beautiful white bird.

'Where are we going?' asked Robert.

'I'm going to show you some things you have never seen before. Then I will take you home,' said Jemma.

Suddenly Jemma flew downwards quickly. Robert had to hold on tightly as they flew towards a huge fish.

'It's a whale!' he cried.

Robert was excited. The whale was so huge and graceful and its dark skin glistened in the water. The albatross circled around it, then it raced very quickly across the surface of the sea so that Robert could see some wonderful dolphins leaping out of the water.

They flew past a boat. Robert waved and called out hello to the children on board who waved back and smiled. The adults looked very worried and told him to come on board. But Jemma flew away again up into the blue sky towards a plane. She beat her wings very quickly and they caught up to it and Robert waved to the passengers who looked out their window and were very surprised to see a little boy waving at them.

Jemma was tired, so she circled down to a tiny island in the middle of the sea. Robert went exploring. There were beautiful beaches of white sand and tall palm trees. He climbed to the top of the island and found a huge hole. It looked like it went right through the centre of the earth. And far, far away he could see a light.

Robert was a very adventurous boy. He told Jemma about the hole and the two of them flew back to it.

'Where do you think it goes?' asked Robert.

'Shall we have a look?' suggested Jemma.

'How?' asked Robert.

'I'll fly,' said Jemma.

So the two of them flew down into the hole. They flew on and on and on. It got hotter and hotter. It was the centre of the earth. About them were huge caves filled with boiling magma. It gurgled and plopped like golden mud.

As they flew through and away from the centre, the light got larger and closer and just when they were getting tired again they flew out of the hole. Up into the air towards the gray clouds.

They looked down and saw a city.

'Where are we?' asked Jemma.

Robert looked around him and saw a huge river and a huge bridge and a massive dome.

'That's St Paul's Cathedral!' yelled Robert. 'We're in London!'

He remembered all the buildings from a book he had read. They flew over the Houses of Parliament and beside Big Ben and Nelson's Column in Trafalgar Square.

'We've flown to the other side of the world!' yelled Robert, he was so excited.

They saw Harrods and museums and art galleries and all the people shopping in Oxford Street. There were so many people going about in different directions and hundreds of cars driving through the roads.

'We have to take back some gold,' said Robert.

'What for?' asked Jemma.

'Because the streets of London are paved with gold and I have to take some back for my mummy and daddy to show them where we've been.'

They flew to Covent Garden where there were all sorts of interesting people and wonderful things to buy. Jemma came down to land but Robert couldn't find any gold. He reached down but the cobbles were just concrete. He was very sad. The books had said they were made of gold. Then a twinkle caught his eye and he saw a small ring sitting in the cracks.

'Look!' he cried. 'Gold!'

Robert was very happy and he got back onto Jemma and took off again. As they flew over London, Robert waved to all the people who pointed and looked amazed because they had never seen an albatross before. And they certainly hadn't seen one with a little boy sitting on it.

They found the hole and flew back to the centre of the earth and through to the other side, back to their little island and their families.'

I stopped talking and the children just sat there, their eyes and mouths wide open.

Then one of them stood up.

'Tell us another story, Charlie!'

'Yes, tell us another story,' they all agreed, and started clapping in anticipation.

'Ah, now children, I think that's enough stories for now. Let's all say thank you to Charlie for such a wonderful story,' said the clown.

'More stories, please!'

'But then we won't have another story for tomorrow.'

'Please!'

They were adamant, but the mothers sensed this was their moment and they moved in to pick up their children, thanking us and looking forward to seeing us tomorrow.

I stayed sitting there, the clown joining me.

'It's been a long time, Charles.'

I turned to him, not having a clue who he was.

'Let me take off this outfit.'

He took off his red nose, rubbed the make-up off his face, scruffled up his hair and turned back to face me.

It took a few seconds.

'Lionel!'

'That's right.'

'You're a clown!'

'And so are you now.'

'You're a clown? How long have you been a clown?'

'Oh, let me see, 1995, summer 1995, so five years.'

'Why?'

'I saw a clown one day and I thought, that's what I really want to do, make children laugh.'

'But how do you survive? They didn't pay you.'

'I don't need much. What more do I need than those smiles, everyone loves a clown.'

'I would never have guessed. You were brilliant at law.'

He stood, preparing to leave.

'I'll see you tomorrow,' said Lionel.

'I'd love to, but ...'

'Hey Charles, the children loved your story, and you made that up on the spot. That's all they need, we're all they've got to make their lives special.'

He looked serious.

'I'll see you tomorrow.'

I nodded, I would be back tomorrow.

I was hungry now, I had to find some food. I selected a sandwich at Somerfield. It was made of white bread, tuna and was absurdly thin. I thought it was ridiculous anyone would eat such a pathetic morsel as I stood in the queue along with a dozen others buying their morsels.

'How are you today?' asked the girl at the checkout.

'I'm well, thank you. And how are you?'

'Just got a raise, so I'm very happy.'

'Excellent!'

She smiled. She was a plain girl standing behind the counter in a plain supermarket. Her makeup was cheap and had been put on too thickly. Her lipstick was pink, her uniform absurdly unfashionable, but her name badge said Mary and she was genuinely happy.

'What are you going to spend the money on?'

'I'm going to buy my little boy a scooter, he loves them, been wanting one for ages, and I get paid on Thursday, so I'll nip off before the shops close and buy him one.'

'Good for you.'

Normally I would stop talking then, well no, normally I would have stopped at 'I'm well, thank you,' but I carried on, wanting to know more.

'How old's your boy?'

'Eight.'

'He must run you round.'

'Oh he does, don't you worry. He's a right scoundrel. But he's a great kid, plays footie. He's good, a striker. He scored loads of goals this season for school. I went to every game.'

'You're very proud of him.'

'Yes I am, Aaron, he's my boy.'

I smiled and thanked her for the sandwich. I had held up the queue but they didn't seem to mind.

I had lunch on a bench, watching others race past me. Lunchtime seemed to be a very busy time of day when you were supposed to be taking a break.

It was one o'clock and I realised I hadn't organised the books for the eight old dears. I really had to think of a better name for them. All sorts of ideas floated round my mind as I headed off to the office.

I wandered in just as normal. It wasn't until the others started looking at me a little oddly that I knew something was wrong.

I stuck my head round Tim's door.

'Charles!'

He paused.

'What on earth …'

I didn't have a clue what was the matter.

'I'll put this simply Charles, you look dreadful.'

'Do I?'

'I knew you were doing the poor thing, but really...'

'What's the matter?'

'Come with me.'

Tim gestured and I duly followed to the bathroom.

'There!'

I looked at the mirror, looked again, then smiled.

'I'm a little ragged.'

'You look dreadful.'

'Really?'

'Really.'

I winced at my reflection.

'I do, don't I?'

'Where did you sleep last night?'

'On your bench.'

'My bench?'

'On the canal. Where you met Jenny.'

'That wasn't even comfortable to sit on. You could have gone home and had a shower.'

'Not quite the plan, I'm learning how to be poor.'

'That doesn't mean you have to look ugly. Tell you what, why don't we donate the office shower to your poverty, have it as a donation to the cause.'

'That would be great.'

'And what about clothes? Yours are looking pretty awful already.'

'They'll probably get worse.'

'Hmm. Well, have a shower.'

It was a great shower. I stayed under the warm water for ages, thoroughly enjoying it.

Then I went to my office and picked up several books. Tim poked his head round the door, raising his eyebrows, querying what I was doing. He really did have expressive eyebrows.

'They're for the Chanel Girls.'

Tim's eyebrows became even more expressive.

'They all used to be models in the '50s, and I promised them some books to read. We don't need them, we've got too many books in this office as it is.'

'Sure.'

'And there's a few people who might appreciate using the shower, let's face it, we never use it. I'll get them to come in first thing in the morning, they won't cause any fuss.'

'Sure.'

'Now I've got to take these to the Chanel Girls. I promised them I'd be back today so I'd better get a wriggle on.'

I reached the door.

'Must have dinner with you and Jenny soon. All still going well?'

'Very well.'

'Excellent!'

And with that I was off, leaving a bemused looking Tim standing at his office door. It wasn't really fair just turning up like that, but he'd see the funny side of it and make it much more exciting as he recounted it over dinner.

The door to the Chanel Girls' house was unlocked. I made my way into the dark corridor and up the creaking stairs. I knocked at the door.

'Come in,' came a call from within.

I entered, smiling.

'Charles!'

They abandoned their knitting. I had found out yesterday they always knitted between two and four in the afternoon, little jackets and pullovers for Sudan. Apparently they had met a man from there once and there were lots of children who needed clothes in the winters, so they knitted every afternoon and sent them off in a huge bundle every two months.

'You've brought us books, you're a marvel!'

They leapt out of bed and crowded round the books I laid on the table. They were enthralled, flicking from one to another, clambering to find the one they wanted to start with, then they made a final selection and hurried back to bed.

'Thank you, Charles,' said Diane, giving me a gorgeous smile. 'Something to read in the small hours when none of us can sleep.'

'Terrible bind not being able to sleep,' added Rita. 'Sit around all day and sit around all night.'

'We switch off the lights, we just can't sleep. Little naps here and there.'

'So we share our stories from when we were younger.'

'What a life we led.'

'What a life we led!' they all agreed.

They opened their books, adjusted their glasses and began reading. It seemed to be my cue to leave.

I turned.

'You really are wonderful bringing these for us,' said Jemma. 'Please come back next week. Don't forget about us.'

'I won't forget.'

'Thank you.'

Chapter Eighteen

I had to write some articles about the artists. I got out their details and figured I may as well start with the nearest. So Michael it was, in Childers Street, Brent. I started off with no plan, just thought I would have a look and see if I could find an angle.

It wasn't until I was wandering along between the buildings in the estate that I realised it might not be the safest place to walk by myself. A group of lads were lingering, staring, their eyes hard and accusing. What would I do if I was attacked? Run, no, that would be futile, they were only 16 or 17, they'd easily catch me. Shout, hope someone would come. Try and reason with them. I was becoming paranoid. I could hear footsteps behind me. Would they really believe my story that I was here to write an article about a local artist? Not likely! I was a white well dressed male in an urban slum, a prime target for robbery, battery, worse. Except I wasn't.

I stopped and stared at myself. My clothes were crumpled and, although I had showered, I hadn't shaved at the office. I didn't look great.

I turned away from them and ignored their taunts. I was a nobody in their world, they had no interest in me. I carried on until I found the building. I expected gray walls, graffiti and rubbish on the floor. But instead the floors were spotless, the brick walls were recently painted a crisp off-white and along the corridor to the lift were cityscapes from around the world. There were dozens of them, all of them using brilliant colours, heightening the scenes so that the wall was bursting with vitality and life.

I entered the lift which was an underworld fantasy covered in paintings of fish, mermaids and sailors. The buttons were coated in glitter and the roof of the lift appeared transparent with sunlight bursting through the surface of the sea.

I got out on the fourth floor, now in an English countryside. Room 407 was what I was looking for, down the corridor. There were no numbers on the other doors which seemed a bit odd. But there it was, gray, old, graffiti, so out of place with the rest of the floor.

I knocked on the door.

'It's open.'

Not exactly the undoing of several chains and deadlocks I'd been expecting.

I entered and there before me was a huge, and I mean huge room filled with easels and benches and open cupboards with hundreds of supplies, everything you could dream of as an artist. A stereo was playing music loudly and twenty or so young people were working at the easels and benches. They had ripped out the walls of the other flats on the floor and made one vast studio. In amongst it all was Michael, moving from one artist to another, discussing, demonstrating, encouraging. I just stood and watched, amazed. Fans whirled in the ceiling, lights were hung at all sorts of angles, finished works filled the entire far wall. It was a 20th century urban salon.

Michael hurried over.

'Charles, so good of you to come.'

Normally I would have come out with something witty, interesting, but I was so amazed at what was happening I could only smile and shake his hand.

'I'll show you around.'

He introduced me to every artist, taking his time, getting them to discuss their work, what they were endeavouring to achieve, their progress, their future ambitions.

They knew so much, they weren't just kids off the street playing with art instead of a football, this was a genuine art school.

'They blow your mind, don't they?'

'And you created this?'

'Everyone called me crazy.'

'Do they still call you crazy?'

He laughed.

'I enjoy being crazy.'

We discussed the history of the project, how he had graduated and immediately moved into the estate, determined to fulfil a vision he had had at art school.

He had used all his contacts, most of whom were wealthy family friends, and begged enough money to buy up the flats on the floor and demolish them all.

'I wanted to have an amazing space for these kids to work in. I wanted it to be somewhere unique, that they could own, that would be theirs. And I wanted to get hundreds of them involved, to change their world, to rediscover their cultures, to lift their minds away from this grotty estate and inspire them to recreate their world.'

'And you've succeeded.'

'I've succeeded in starting. But there's so much more to do. We've formed a trust and we now have four studios around London with three more planned. These kids are inspiring themselves and inspiring their friends. They don't just talk about the telly and footie anymore, they're discovering their histories, the stories from their parents and their grandparents and they're painting them, celebrating them. They know who they are because they know where they're from. And now that I've got the money from the auction we're going to hold a huge exhibition. I've just got agreement to hold it in Leicester Square. The Mayor of London's going to open it and we're going to have huge publicity, entertainment, food, you name it, and a black tie dinner for the artists.'

I just smiled, a huge beaming smile, there was nothing to add, nothing to say. Michael had taken hold of a dream and through sheer willpower had made it happen.

'Your article will be really beneficial. We need to establish credibility in the art world. I don't want to be seen as a charity, couldn't think of anything worse. These kids are training to be professional artists.'

So I would need more information. My brain stopped being overwhelmed and kicked into gear. We spent an hour discussing his project. I knew that to get it down on paper was going to be easy, it was a story that told itself.

'Why don't you have dinner with me tonight?' he asked.

'Sure, I'd love to.'

We left the artists to their work and wandered out to the main street. Catching a taxi, we headed towards South Kensington.

'I hope you're not too fussy, my wife Mags and I are both useless in the kitchen. We tend to eat out, it's so much easier, but we've got some friends from Cornwall staying and it's nice to lounge around.'

I nodded my head as we turned onto Fulham Road and then into the Little Boltons where we pulled up outside an imposing pillared entrance.

Opening the door, Michael called out he was home. No one responded.

'Probably out the back.'

And they were, only it wasn't just another couple, there were six people lounged around on deck chairs in the garden.

'Darling!' called out Mags, getting up to kiss her husband. 'Lovely to see you home so early.'

He gave her a kiss, short enough not to be embarrassing for onlookers, but long enough to know they thoroughly enjoyed each other's company.

'I invited a few people for dinner.'

'The more the merrier, let's do the introductions.'

There was Stephen the local vicar, Mary and John who lived down in Tregunter Road, and Annabel and David, the couple from Cornwall.

'Charles has been good enough to agree to write an article about the Project in *ArtsNow*.'

They welcomed me warmly, offered a drink, and I joined them. Stephen was the vicar of St Mary's, the church in the middle of the Boltons who had such an interest in art he took himself on a pilgrimage each year around the monasteries of Italy and Spain. Mary and John were both journalists for the

BBC, Mary focussed on politics, John on technology. Annabel and David were sculptors. I knew their work, most in my world did.

'So Charles, you're a journalist?'

'Well, no, not as such. I used to write, bit rusty now, but I'm thoroughly enjoyed seeing Michael's work.'

'So what else do you get up to?' asked Mags.

I almost said 'I'm being poor', but it suddenly seemed absurd, self indulgent, ridiculous. To say that in Michael's company was just plain wrong. It denigrated his students, the extraordinary people I had met who were more fulfilled, more purposeful than I had ever been. It implied that I could just stop using my money and take on the attributes of the poor. But I didn't have their attributes, I was nothing compared to the people I had met over the past few days.

'I am writing a novel.'

'Really?'

'Just in its early stages.'

I paused, the idea taking form in my head.

'Tell us more.'

'Well, there is a painting by *van Gogh*, three figures near a canal walking away from the viewer across a barren landscape towards the horizon. And my novel is about a man who is standing alone behind the three figures and is so intrigued by them he wants to know who they are and where they are going.'

'And will he find out?' asked Stephen.

'I don't know. I hope so.'

'But how do you know they are walking to the horizon?' asked Mags. 'I know the painting, it's in the National Gallery and I've always wondered, what if they aren't on a journey, what if they've arrived at their destination and are going to sit down beside the canal and have a cup of tea and read some poetry?'

'Mags loves playing games, no artist is safe when she's around,' said Michael.

'But a good point,' chipped in Stephen. 'We're always searching for something else when it's often on our doorstep.'

'The grass is greener on the other side.'

'When it's been sprayed with pesticide.'

'Or they could just be going for a pleasant walk in the countryside,' said Annabel. 'They might not be searching at all.'

'It's just three people going for a walk, they aren't running away or searching for anything.'

'Walking gives you time to see people, the surroundings.'

'Gives you a chance to appreciate,' said Stephen.

'And stop often, enjoy it, take time over the little things.'

'*van Gogh's* early paintings weren't about being poor, they were about the people he knew. He just happened to know poor people. If he had been rich he would have painted rich people.'

'There are as many life changing people who are poor as there are rich, and as many dull people who are poor as are rich,' said John.

'I always thought poor people were different,' I said, slowly.

'Until you met one?'

'Yes.'

'And were they any different?'

'Some seem to be very different.'

'As are some with money. You're defining individuals by something that doesn't define them as people,' said Mary.

'Tell me Charles,' said Stephen, leaning forward. 'Why did you decide to become poor?'

'Because I saw a girl die and everyone, and I mean everyone, seemed to care about her death.'

'And what was she doing when she died?'

'She was giving food to the poor.'

'And would they have loved her if she hadn't given them food?'

'They wouldn't have known her.'

'So if you don't do anything for others, will anyone care if you live or die?'

'Only friends and family.'

'So her life had greater meaning than, say, yours?'

'Maybe.'

I smiled, now embarrassed. What did I do compared to that girl and Michael? Work seemed so indulgent, and it could cope without me. My friends could survive without meeting me for dinner. The opera and theatre weren't going to fall to pieces because I didn't renew my subscriptions. The only thing I was doing that was of any use to anyone else was what I had organised over the last few days, dropping books off to the Chanel Girls, telling a story as Charlie the Clown, and writing articles to promote the work of young artists.

'I have a few things.'

'Marvellous!' beamed Mags. 'Now enough of this rather

serious conversation, let's descend on the kitchen and see if we can find anything to eat.'

There was nothing edible, so Mags phoned for takeaways. The wine was poured and laughter and stories started flowing. It was a marvellous evening.

'I feel like some chocolate,' proclaimed John, after finishing off his meal.

'There's none here,' winced Michael. 'We must work on stocking our pantry, it takes up such a lot of room for virtually no purpose.'

'I could go and get some,' offered Stephen.

I glanced at my watch. It was 11.30.

'I'm afraid I've got to go,' I said.

'Do you want to sleep here tonight?' asked Mags.

'That would be great, but no I'm off to visit Steve to start work on his article.'

'Of course, he works in the middle of the night,' said Michael. 'I've been wanting to catch up with him for ages, why don't I come with you?'

'If you're sure.'

'Sure I'm sure. We'll take the car, pick up some chocolate first of course, then we'll drive on over.'

Chapter Nineteen

Peckham Common in the middle of the night was not somewhere I'd ever expected to be. It was asking for trouble, but Michael got out of the car, filled with the anticipation of seeing Steve's work.

'We won't miss it.'

We walked quickly down the path, turned a couple of corners, passed through a gate, and entered the Common.

'Don't turn around until I say so.'

We walked about fifty yards.

'Now.'

I turned slowly and my eyes literally widened. Four of the buildings were covered in shimmering, soft, subtle light. It was a mosaic of light, reds and yellows and oranges, softer at the bottom and brighter at the tops of the buildings. They were flames and were moving as if gently in the breeze.

I stood speechless for a couple of minutes, absolutely lost for words, mesmerised by the gentle movement of the flames.

'How?' I whispered.

'Come closer and you'll see.'

They were bulbs, each of them emitting a different coloured light for a different period of time.

'How do they work?'

'For that you'll need to speak with Steve, he's the genius.'

We made our way up the elevator to the third level of one of the buildings.

'In here.'

Michael pushed open an unlocked door and we entered. The entire room was a mass of gadgets, of wiring, lights and computers. In the midst of it all was Steve, intently altering one of the hundreds of lights.

'Michael! Charles!'

He leapt to his feet, knocking several objects to the floor, not worrying, stepping over them, and extended his hand in welcome.

'So good of you to come. I'm making some great progress.'

'I saw your lights outside.'

'It's looking fantastic!'

'Isn't it? The team work so hard. We're hoping to put up another two floors tonight.'

'The team?'

'Oh, they're across in what we call the warehouse. I'll introduce you.'

We descended a flight of steps and entered the first door. It was just like Michael's studio in that several flats had been demolished to form a single room, but this one was filled with literally thousands and thousands of lights.

Scattered about were a dozen teenagers all working intensely, sorting and counting.

'We do a lot of checking in here before we mount them.'

'It must take hours.'

'Weeks, but they love it. Every night they arrive at work and see what they have achieved. They can't believe it's theirs.'

He explained what each person's task was and how it

would fit into the completed whole when they fixed them to the walls, then he switched the lights on and off twice and his team turned to look at him.

'Are we all go for stage 63?' he asked, signing.

They all yelled 'yes,' in various tones.

'They're deaf?' I asked.

'Of course, didn't you know?'

'No, I had no idea.'

'Oh, sorry, I just forget, I'm so used to it. Right, let's go.'

They loaded their piles of lights into wheelbarrows and headed off down the corridor, then down the lift one at a time and along to a half lit building.

'I've only seen this once,' said Michael. 'You're in for a treat.'

They drove their barrows into the building and there was silence. We stood and waited.

Then, from the top of the building, six ropes dropped to the ground and, completely silently, people appeared, abseiling down the building. A dark rope with objects on it trailed behind them.

They stopped three stories up and, one by one, they took hold of an object on the string and activated it to become a shining light.

It was so quiet, such an extraordinary sight. The lights were put on unbelievably quickly, the figures crawling over the building, the flame growing higher and higher. I was so absorbed it wasn't until I heard a cough behind me that I realised there were others around us. I turned, there were dozens standing silently, watching, their eyes filled with the growing light of the flame.

Then they finished and the silent figures crawled back up the building, disappearing over the edge of the roof, the ropes following them.

I stayed watching the almost finished flame, wanting it to be completed, wanting to see the tip, but that was all there was for that night. I would have to come back, as would the others who had gathered to watch.

We turned away as silently as the workers, and I walked beside Michael back onto the estate.

Inside the warehouse there was pandemonium, they were celebrating!

'It's like this every night we put up the lights,' yelled Steve. 'We work for weeks on the lights so when we get them up it's really exciting. Come and meet everyone.'

It was a fantastic couple of hours. His team had three sets of drums and all sorts of disco lights, flashing in rhythm. We danced and laughed. I was taught a few basic words of sign language and Steve outlined how a light worked. I didn't understand it at all, but I smiled and was genuinely impressed.

They gradually drifted away and Michael and I made our farewells, wandering out to have a final look at the flames on the buildings.

There were a few others there, standing silently watching. I would normally have walked on quickly, worried about being mugged, but there was something about the lights that made me feel safe, like this was a safe place to stand and enjoy the beauty of the lights and the stars in the sky above.

Chapter Twenty

My bones were sore when I woke the next morning on the bench by the canal. I didn't care, the sun was just rising and the canal was a fairy wonderland below the light blue sky. The ducks swam in a straight line towards the park under the trees that drooped down to the water.

I sat up and ran my fingers through my hair as an old man ambled towards me.

'Beautiful day,' he offered.

'It is indeed,' I agreed.

He shuffled past, his shoes scraping the footpath, with shoulders slightly bent and arms hardly moving.

A girl cycled towards him. Seeing him she stopped, jumped off the bike and gave him a hug. He suddenly became a different man, standing tall, animated, laughing with her. They talked for a few minutes, then he gave her a kiss on the cheek and carried on.

'Good morning,' she said, coming to a stop beside me, setting her bike against the chair.

'Another gorgeous day.'

I wondered if she had ever walked on water, if that was something angels could do, or if that was reserved just for God.

'Fancy some breakfast?'

She reached into her bag and brought out some freshly baked croissants and cheese and a bottle of orange juice, laying them on a table cloth between us on the bench.

'Here you go.'

'Thank you!'

It was truly delicious.

'This is the way to wake up.'

'Out in the fresh air.'

We sat and ate, enjoying the food and the surroundings.

'Would you like to meet some of my friends?' asked the girl.

'Love to,' I replied. 'Although I should probably find out your name first.'

'My name is Amy.'

'Really?'

'What's wrong with Amy?'

'Nothing, just, I thought it might be something a little more unusual, you know, given who you are.'

'And who am I?' she smiled.

'I assume you are an angel.'

'Really?' she laughed. 'An angel!'

'Well you are, aren't you?'

'No, why do you think I'm an angel?'

'The four leafed clover and what you were saying last time we met.'

'I just happened to find a four leafed clover.'

'And you gave it away?'

'I didn't need it.'

'And I did?'

'Yes, I think you did.'

'So you really work at the pet shop?'

'I'm just an ordinary girl.'

'Ah well, there we go, I'll still think of you as an angel.'

'Then come with me and meet some of my friends.'

We finished breakfast then walked down the High Street, past the shops that were opening.

'In here.'

She pushed the buzzer and the door to the building opened. There was a tidy foyer with offices on either side.

A man appeared, smiling.

'Amy, lovely to see you.'

She gave him a hug and introduced me to Phil, the manager of the hostel.

'Nicest guy in the world,' she whispered, loudly enough for Phil to hear.

'She says that about everyone,' he laughed. 'Coffee?'

He made coffee in the kitchen, filling the room with a fantastic aroma.

'Nothing like a good coffee to kick-start your day. Why don't we go through to my office? We shouldn't get disturbed too often.'

'Everyone needs you, Phil.'

He swiftly gathered up piles of documents off the chairs and stacked them high on his desk.

'The Council wants to know what we're up to. I try to tell them we're too busy doing things to write reports about what we're doing, but they still want the paperwork and as they give us the money, hey, another late night.'

We all sat down.

'So Charles, I hear you're in the book business.'

I smiled, realising he knew I was coming

'Yes, Phil, I dabble a little.'

'It must an exciting industry to be involved in.'

'It has its moments.'

'And you've written yourself?'

'I was a journalist some time ago.'

'So you've been on both sides of the fence.'

'The grass is green on both sides.'

'I've never been able to write myself other than these awful reports. I've thought about it, I even started a couple of times, but didn't get past the first page. I could never get excited about what I was writing.'

'Certainly isn't for everyone.'

'Fun though, for a couple of days pretending I was going to be a famous novelist with reviews in the newspapers, and interviews on the radio. Ah well, I shall just have to keep this place going.'

'Where would we be without you?' asked Amy.

Phil smiled, he was as mesmerised by Amy as I was.

'Shall I show you around?'

'Lead on, Phil.'

I still hadn't been asked to do anything. This was disconcerting. I must have been brought here for a reason, to contribute, to do something for nothing, that was how charities operated. I'd played the game for years, giving freebees. But perhaps this was different.

We walked through the hostel. There were thirty three beds, one per room, all female.

'Most have some dependency,' whispered Phil. 'Drugs, alcohol. And of course you can't have dependency without associated mental health problems, so we have a number of counsellors and psychologists who visit.'

'Have they stopped using?'

'Some have, some haven't. We're not a rehab, we provide a place for them to get off the street.'

'So they use drugs in the hostel?'

'We're here to give advice, help, guidance, and get them into shared housing or rehab if that's what's appropriate. But for some of them it isn't possible at this stage. We look after our girls, we don't judge them.'

The hostel was sparkling clean. There was artwork on the corridors, most of them originals.

'Here's the library.'

Phil opened a large room and it was jam packed with books from the floor to the ceiling.

'Wow! There must be thousands of books here.'

'The girls love reading.'

'How do you lend them? It must be a nightmare making sure they all get back.'

'We don't have a system. The books are here for them. They can read them whenever, wherever they want, there's no rules. If they love a book, they're free to keep it.'

We continued on up to the kitchen where a couple of women were making breakfast. They greeted us with warm smiles as they were introduced.

There were plates and utensils neatly in drawers and stacked on shelves. I noticed a couple of large knives sitting on cutting boards.

I pointed them out quietly to Phil. He nodded and we left the kitchen.

'There is no violence here. The girls come from a sad world and this is their haven, they look out for each other. We don't have any locks, the wardrobes are open in the bedrooms. They don't have anything when they come here, that's why they're here. So we don't treat them like prisoners. This is their world where they can regain their self respect.'

We carried on down the corridor to a door that opened into a lounge. Inside were a dozen women sitting in a circle.

'This is our poetry circle where they share the poems they have written over the past week. Would you like to have a listen? They really are very good.'

I felt like an intruder as Phil warmly introduced me and Amy was greeted by the others.

None of the women were the same. They were all different ages, shapes, ethnicities, but they were obviously friends, discussing people they knew, what had been going on in their lives.

'It's lovely you are here, Charles. Do you write poetry?' asked Jo, the co-ordinator of the group.

I shook my head.

'Yes he does,' said Amy.

I smiled, but shook my head even more firmly.

'He does,' said Amy. 'Do you want to read it or me?'

She was unfolding a few pieces of typed paper.

'Where did you find that?'

'Google is a wonderful thing.'

'I didn't know ...'

'Why don't you read it, Charles? Be great if you could start us off this morning.'

Amy passed me the paper and I recognised it as something I had had published years before.

'This is from a long time ago.'

'Some of us are older than you. I'll read something from when I was young after you if that makes you feel better,' laughed Jo. 'That will be truly ancient literature.'

The others urged me on. I was hesitant, I wasn't sure if I wanted to own it. But they kept on until I had to give in.

'The first one is called *The Dimly Lit Café*. I must have been 18 when I wrote this so you'll have to excuse me.'

'Just read it,' said Amy quietly.

'Okay, here goes …

A glass door, framed by peeling white paint,
And smeared by the dull, monotonous drifts of rain
Opened, slowly, to reveal a girl sitting,
Alone, in a dimly lit café.

Tall, graceful, elegant,
Her long dark hair effortlessly draped
About the pale delicacy of her face.
A coffee lingered beside a paperback,
And the blueness of her eyes,
Dulled by the sadness of the city,
Stared into the pale greyness of the world outside.

Finally, she glanced down at the words of the book,
And slowly, so slowly, as time itself dissolved
And the city about her faded,
Her spirit could once more remember a story of love,
Of beauty,
Of Alexandria,
Of a world that had awoken her, overwhelmed her.

Her eyes flickered,
Their startling blue now awash with the memories
Of the cafés, the markets,
The people, the lovers, the dreamers,
Of a time she had been at one with them,
And she smiled, an exquisite moment of such beauty,
That the Spirit of God,
Settled upon the towers of the Notre Dame,
Was stirred from slumber,
And the sadness rose once more from the city.'

I finished and the women smiled and clapped and insisted I read some more.

'I'm sure someone else would like a turn?'

But there was no stopping them.

'Okay, well seeing you asked for them, here they are. But this is it, there's only three poems here and I can't even remember writing them so I can't vouch they're any good. I certainly wouldn't publish them.'

They just kept smiling in anticipation.

I gave up.

'Here you go then. The next one is called *A Photograph.*

Hurried footsteps below me,
shoes clicking on cobblestones,
people's faces blurring,
cars slowly edging,
birds fluttering,
all beyond, outside me,

merely a backdrop,
nothing in particular.
The lighted sign grows brighter, closer,
enticing, exciting,
welcoming me into the shop.
A girl takes my money and hands me a package.
My fingers rush to open,
my eyes focussing,
my heart racing,
the photo before me.
She is smiling under the perfected brightness
of a Moroccan sky,
the stalls are filled with fruit, spices, radiant people.
Happiness overwhelms me, I am a slave to this, to her,
to the life that excites within her world.
I turn, never to return,
the photographs now a mosaic upon the concrete,
memories of the life that will always be mine.
They call to others, to leave the dull greyness
and join me, joining her,
under that distant Moroccan sky.

And the last one is called *Smoke*. I didn't really go overboard
on the titles, did I?

Smoke hung about the café, gently folding upon itself,
sneaking up behind friends and lovers,
eavesdropping on their conversations,
whispering comments into their ears,
bouncing on their laughter,

gliding on their sighs,
sampling their food and drink.
Then it slid across to the corner of the room,
taking the moments of their lives,
and soared into the freezing cold air, past the dark bricks,
the lighted windows, the multitude of chimneys,
away above the clouds where,
amidst the startling brightness of the stars,
it met with friends and danced with the joy
of all it had tasted and heard.

So there you are, poems from another lifetime.'

'And have you changed?' asked Jo.

I didn't respond, I hadn't anticipated discussing the poems. It was embarrassing enough having to read them. I just smiled.

'They sound like you want to live somewhere else, escape, like the world you live in doesn't make you happy,' said Pip.

''Like you can't accept what is in the here and now. You haven't come to terms with your own world.'

'You're like the smoke, drifting in and out, not staying in the room. Taking what you need and then leaving.'

'An illusion, that's what Morocco and Alexandria are. They aren't real, are they? You hadn't visited them when you wrote the poetry, had you?'

'No, I hadn't.'

'So they were somewhere you created in your mind, based on something you read perhaps?'

'Maybe.'

'Your Neverland where you could escape, but you never

actually flew out the window, the smoke stayed in the room, didn't it? You stayed in the room and dreamed of somewhere else.'

'You never committed yourself to the room, to the people around you. Your mind wanted to belong to something more exotic.'

'So you never fully experienced the world in which you lived because you never committed yourself to it?' asked Jo.

'The grass is greener on the other side but we never eat all the grass in our own field.'

'Always searching, journeying, when we could just stop and open our eyes a little wider.'

'Instead of searching?' I asked.

'We don't need to search, we just need to stand still and experience, otherwise we are so intent on the journey we don't discover what is right in front of us.'

'Like we've got blinkers on that only show us the horizon.'

'So we don't see the ground we're standing on.'

'I know it sounds silly, but I've been searching for what it means to be poor.'

They all burst into laughter.

'No, no, I'm serious, I've been living on a park bench and …'

I couldn't keep going, they were in fits of laughter.

'Darling,' said Jo. 'You may as well count the sand on the seashore. Us poor lot are so different there's no such thing as *being poor*.'

'I thought if I didn't have money I would discover a different world, and I have!'

'That's not because you haven't got money, that's because you've bothered to open your eyes. You're just looking for something more.'

'I know there's more.'

'Well you don't need to be poor to discover that. You can be rich or poor. Look at Phil, does he have any money? Do we care? We all love him, why? Because he's real, he's not hiding anything, not trying to be someone he isn't. He devotes his life to people like us who need a helping hand, and that's why we respect him. Use your money, use your skills, don't give them up. Accept who you are and what you've achieved. Then find something to commit yourself to, give it your all, and then you won't need to search.'

'I have no idea what to commit to.'

'Then open your eyes a little wider.'

Amy smiled.

'Poor Charles. I brought him here to listen to your poetry and he's been ambushed.'

'Yes I have, very unfair!'

'They call us *The Crazy Camden Circle.*'

'So do you stay at this hostel?'

'Lynn does. The rest of us have been in and moved on, but we love to visit and read poems and see Phil.'

'It's the highlight of my week,' said Pip.

'Well, I want to hear some of your poems now.'

'With pleasure!'

Chapter Twenty One

I got so caught up in the poetry I forgot I was booked to be
Charlie the Clown. I excused myself from sharing a cup of
tea and hurried off. The children were laughing and
shouting, demanding a differently shaped balloon. One of
the boys turned as I approached.

'There's Charlie!'

'Charlie!'

They ran towards me, crowded round my legs and gave
me a big hug.

'It's time I learnt your names,' I said loudly over their
enthusiastic greeting.

They yelled them all at once.

'No, no, I need to hear them one at a time, and something
about you, like what's your favourite game, or what's the
yummiest thing to eat in all the world.'

They stood back and, still huffing and puffing with
excitement, they rushed around the group giving their
names and their favourite food and football team.

'Do you like stories?'

'Yes!' they yelled back.

'Are you sure you like stories?'

'Yes! Yes! Yes!' they yelled even louder. 'Tell us a story,
tell us a story!!!'

You could say I was milking the crowd I was enjoying
them so much, they were such gorgeous kids, so open and
wanting to love and be loved.

'Do you want me to tell you a story?'

'Yes! Yes! Yes! Tell us a story Charlie!'

'All right then, but you'll have to sit down nicely.'

Immediately they sat in a circle around my feet. I sat down with them, strangely wanting to get nearer, to let their enthusiasm, their love for life rub off on me.

'Have you heard the story about the little girl who went to Marshmallow Land?'

'No!'

'Perhaps I should tell you that one then?'

'Pleeeease Charlie.'

'Well, once upon a time, not so very long ago …'

'How long ago?' asked Shanelle.

'Three years, two months, and one day.'

'I'm four,' declared Shanelle.

'Really?'

The rest then chimed in with how old they were.

'You're not very old are you?'

'No,' they said, concentrating.

'Well, the little girl was the same age as you when she walked down the path outside her new house one day. She was being a little bit naughty because her parents had asked her not to walk that way by herself and she knew she would be in trouble when they found out.'

'You shouldn't do naughty things,' said Freddy.

'No you shouldn't,' I agreed, casting a quick reassuring glance towards the parents.

'Anyway, she was being very careful, not walking near any cars or anything dangerous.'

'What was her name?'

'Lucy.'

'My name's Lucy,' said Lucy, beaming with excitement.

'Yes it is. So Lucy walked down the path near her house in the country which led to a small pond.'

'Were there any ducks?' asked Geoff.

'Yes there were, thirteen ducks.'

'That's a lot of ducks for a small pond.'

'They were small ducks.'

'Special ducks?'

'Special ducks with yellow speckled beaks.'

'I've never heard of yellow speckled beaks,' said Lucy, thinking hard. 'Are you sure they weren't striped?'

'Perhaps they were.'

'Because I've seen ducks with striped beaks.'

'Where?' asked John.

'In a book.'

'What book?'

'The book I've got at home.'

'Are you sure it's a real duck, not just a make believe duck?'

'I don't think ducks have striped beaks.'

'It is true,' said Lucy, indignant, but starting to look upset.

'These ducks definitely had striped beaks,' I said quickly.

That quietened them down for a moment, just long enough for me to wonder why I wasn't upset. Normally being around kids drove me insane, I had a low tolerance for anyone under four feet tall. But I was enjoying myself with this rowdy mob, not getting on with my story and answering all sorts of silly questions.

'So Lucy wandered down the path. It was a little longer

than she expected with lots of twists and turns past large trees and a little river. She came to a fence. Over the fence she could see a beautiful field with fruit trees …'

I carried on the story, making it up as I went, discovering a world of marshmallow people and trees made of sweeties. The children kept interrupting, wanting to know more detail. I kept on going, loving their attention and the world we had entered together, finally returning Lucy to her house, the adventure finished.

The children begged for more, another story, and I wanted to tell them another as much as they wanted to hear one. But it was time for them to go and I waved goodbye to my little friends.

'Aren't they great?'

Lionel was sitting on the ground behind me. I didn't turn, I didn't want him to see the tears in my eyes. They had appeared as the children had walked away, waving, smiling, holding their mothers' hands.

'More than that.'

'Yes, much more than that. I discovered that one day, just like you, and I haven't been able to stop coming here since. They grow up of course and they don't need a silly clown anymore, but others come along.'

'I'll be here.'

'We'll have a lot of fun.'

'Yes we will.'

I wiped the tears from my eyes and stood.

'Thanks Lionel.'

'Don't thank me, thank them. Every day I thank them for coming to see me. If I hadn't met them I would never have been happy. Strange thing happiness, no one talks about it anymore. Everyone wants to be positive and become some extraordinary person with the power of positive thinking and all that, but me, I'm happy, and that's enough.'

'You're an extraordinary person.'

Lionel laughed.

'That's just it, I'm not. I'm as ordinary as they come. I can't even do proper clown tricks, all I can do is make simple balloon animals. Haven't you noticed, they all look pretty well the same? And I don't have an imagination, I can't make up stories like you.'

'But they love you.'

'Yes they love me, and that makes what I do special. It's not about me and what I can do, it's about them. All about them.'

He stood, and for the first time I realised that his clown costume was grubby and torn, his shoes were scuffed with holes.

He turned to go.

'I'll see you again soon?' he asked.

'Yes,' I nodded.

'Great! I'll look forward to hearing another story. Have fun!'

And with that he turned and walked away with a slight limp.

Chapter Twenty Two

It was lunchtime. I knew that because I was feeling hungry. I made my way towards the shops, considering what I would eat.

A man stood outside the tailor's. He didn't say anything, just held out a mug. He wore an old suit, a white shirt, untucked, old shoes on his feet, a crinkled hat, and his face, what I could see of it, was covered in a filthy beard.

I walked past, his stench hitting me. I didn't give him any money, I didn't have enough to give.

I entered the supermarket and glanced at the sandwiches, the cheapest being egg on thin white bread. I took a packet and paid at the counter.

The man was still there when I left. He hadn't moved at all and there was no money in his mug. I walked past him, deliberately quickly.

He shouldn't be there, he stunk. He should be at one of the hostels. They'd give him lunch and a bath, clean him up. He could upset people standing there looking like that.

I turned, I didn't know why. I was fifty yards past him. He should get himself together, there was no excuse. It wouldn't take much to have a bath, to get some new clothes from the second hand shops.

I walked towards him. What was I going to do? Who knows what he had done in the past? He could be a criminal, a molester. He shouldn't be there, not on the main street.

I stopped in front of him. He kept his head down. It was

pathetic, he could at least look up. If he was going to be there, ask for our money, be a nuisance, he should have the guts to show his face.

He looked up and raised his mug slightly towards me.

'Do you want some lunch?' I asked, not intending to, the words just coming out of my mouth.

He kept staring at me.

'Some food?' I asked.

I took the sandwich out of my bag and offered it to him. He raised his hand and touched the packet.

'For me?'

'Yes.'

'Thank you.'

He took the packet and tried to open it, but he didn't have the strength.

I went to help, leaning towards him, the stench stronger, almost too much to bear.

'I'll help you open them,' I said.

I raised my arms slightly showing him my palms, trying to show him he didn't have any reason to fear me.

I stood there for over a minute while he deliberated, then he handed me the packet very quickly.

'What say we share them?' I suggested. 'I'm a bit hungry and this was going to be my lunch.'

I opened the packet and he took the sandwich from my outstretched hand.

'Thank you,' he said.

He sat down on the bench a few feet away. I joined him, still fighting back my revoltion of his stench.

We ate in silence.

'I know I stink.'

'You could probably do with a shower.'

'I don't want to waste water.'

'I see.'

'But you don't, do you?'

I hesitated. There was anger in his voice.

'No, I don't.'

'Then don't say you understand something when you don't.'

'I'm sorry.'

'Are you?'

'Yes, I didn't mean to offend you.'

'Then I accept your apology. Do you want a drink?'

He took a flask out of his jacket pocket.

'No, thanks.'

'Why not?'

'I don't drink at lunchtime.'

'I bet you do.'

I hesitated again. Of course I drank at lunchtime. I would often have a drink with friends for lunch.

'Yes, you're right, I do drink at lunchtime.'

'Then perhaps you would like a drink?'

I shook my head.

'Because this is whisky?'

'A little strong for me.'

'Smell it.'

He thrust it towards me and I was forced to sniff.

'Orange juice,' he said. 'Now would you like some?'

The man was obviously ill, he could have any number of diseases. It wasn't safe to drink out of his flask.

'Yes I'm dying, but I am not infectious. You gave me a sandwich, now I am giving you a drink.'

I took a quick breath to cast aside my fear and I drank the orange juice.

'Thank you.'

'I don't live in a hostel because I used to get violent when I was drunk, so I've been banned. I'm not in hospital because there's nothing they can do to save me.'

'But surely, they …'

'I am an old, ugly, rotten man waiting to die.'

'Is there anything I can do?'

'You have given me lunch.'

'Yes, but, I could …'

'That is enough, thank you.'

He stood, his hand pressing hard, shaking against his cane as he rose.

'It is time for cards. Do you want to play?'

He didn't wait for an answer. He turned slowly and shuffled slowly up the road.

I walked with him, aware of everyone staring at both of us. A girl chewing gum spat it on the ground just as we passed. The old man's steps continued on. He didn't avoid it, he seemed to acknowledge he was worthy of such abuse.

We finally made it to the end of the shops and turned into an alley. There beside a graffitied fence sat three men, their clothes and demeanour the same as the man beside me.

As we approached, they stood, all struggling, shaking, and extended their hands in greeting.

I introduced myself and they welcomed me with thin smiles.

'Poker for the walking dead,' said Jim.

'We play for days,' added Don. 'The more you win the longer you stay alive.'

'We don't try and win,' said my companion, Sammy.

The cards were shuffled slowly and dealt.

'There used to be eight of us.'

The game began. It was the worst game of poker I had ever seen. The participants deliberately lost as they began talking, remembering, talking about old times, friends, relationships, places they had visited, the War, and the lovers who had come and gone, leaving them here with nothing, betting, hastening their deaths.

I sat and listened, intrigued by their stories, appalled at their jokes until the game finally finished and they rose.

'It has been good to meet you Charles,' said Don. 'You must drop by sometime soon and hopefully I won't be here.'

'Or me,' agreed the others.

I opened my mouth to say something, to protest, to argue.

'Charles, we have lived for a long time. All you see are our corpses. Don't think we were always like this. Years ago we were just like you. But we made some wrong choices, we took the wrong road and we can't undo that. But these card games we play, they give us a chance to talk, and as long as we can remember the good times we can die happy.'

'For a few hours a day, we're happy again.'

'That's all we've got, Charles. Our memories.'

Sammy took my hand and shook it, lacking any strength. I shook all their hands, seeing death in their eyes.

'I hope to see you again.'

'Goodbye Charles.'

Chapter Twenty Three

I made my way back to Camden and dropped by the pet shop where Amy was reading at the counter.

'What are you reading?'

'A book about *van Gogh*.'

'Any particular reason?'

'I thought it might be interesting.'

'I just bought a book about *van Gogh*.'

'Perhaps we've got something in common?'

'Perhaps we have.'

I shrugged and smiled, and then she smiled back. That made me wonder. Was she suggesting something more? Was she saying that she … no, don't even start to think it! The most common mistake among us mere mortals is to think girls fancy us when they don't, and the only outcome is embarrassment and a hasty retreat.

'I was passing and thought I'd say hi …'

She smiled again, tilting her head slightly to the side.

'Fancy dinner?'

I paused, seemingly for ages, desperately willing myself to talk.

'Ah, certainly … sure … love to,' I stammered.

'In half an hour when I finish work?'

'Sure, great, I'll be back in a bit.'

'See you then.'

I retreated, smiling, trying to look relaxed, but my heart was pounding. When I got outside I couldn't help but smile.

Then I laughed.

I didn't know what to do. I had half an hour to fill in. I wandered down the street and found everything incredibly interesting. It was like I had walked into another world. The shops I had walked past hundreds of times, the people, even the cracks between the cobblestones seemed fascinating. I knew how silly I was being and I enjoyed it.

Should I get flowers?

Flowers implied this meant something, and it did for me, but not for Amy, another potential embarrassment. Mustn't do flowers.

But what about wild flowers? That was different, it was off the cuff with no financial transaction.

Where could I get them? I only had fifteen minutes. Jess and Andrew, they had flowers, I could just make it. I didn't want to run, well let's face it, I couldn't run, hadn't jogged in years, would probably cripple myself. So a very quick walk. I hadn't walked quickly for ages, never had any need. It fascinated me how long I could make my stride, skipping past people in the way.

They might not be there, then what would I do? Best just to stop, retreat, calm down. But I had the idea in my head now.

Jess was sitting on the back of the houseboat.

'Jess!'

She turned and smiled.

'Hi Charles, lovely to see you. I've got some spare flowers, would you like them?'

I stopped, wondering if she had said that or if I had imagined it.

'Flowers, Charles.'

'Yes please.'

'Here you go. Aren't they beautiful?'

'Yes they are, thank you.'

I half turned, blinking a little too quickly.

'Yes, thank you. Sorry, have to dash, see you again soon.'

'We're having dinner tomorrow.'

'Are we?'

Oops, I shouldn't have said that out loud. Always a mistake to verbalise forgetfulness.

'At your place.'

'My place?'

'We're having dinner on this bench tomorrow night.'

'Marvellous, looking forward to it.'

'Are you okay?'

I stopped.

'Tell you the truth Jess, I think I am.'

I nodded in self agreement.

'But I'd better dash or else I'll be late for something very important. Thank you so much for the flowers.'

I hurried off and made it back to the pet shop three minutes early. It gave me a chance to stand on the corner and catch my breath. I wasn't getting any younger so I had two choices, either never be late or take up jogging and get fit.

It was time to approach the shop, casually, relaxed. Just having dinner, nothing special, a new friend, that was all.

I entered the shop as Amy was coming out. We bumped into each other at the door and the flowers were knocked out of my hand.

'Sorry!'

'Sorry!'

I smiled sheepishly and picked up the flowers.

'I was just passing the, er, and there were some, er, flowers …'

She gave me a kiss on the cheek.

'Thanks Charles, they're gorgeous.'

Girls should never, never kiss a guy on the cheek when he's clearly nervous, it just wasn't fair. I momentarily lost complete control, glazed over, the gentle touch of her lips, the brushing of her hair, her eyes so close. It just wasn't fair!

'Charles.'

Come on, get yourself together, she'll think you're a blithering idiot.

'Sorry, banged my head on the door.'

'Are you okay?'

'I think so.'

I shook my head, getting my mind back in focus. Now concentrate Charles, you know you're useless at first dates and this is definitely a first date. It doesn't matter if Amy thinks it is or not, going into a daze means you think it is. You're going to have to concentrate and not say or do silly things.

'I thought we'd go down to Soho. What do you think?'

'Great idea.'

We caught the tube. It was rush hour so we had to stand very close. I realised she was taller than I'd thought. We didn't say a lot, bit tricky with other people pushed up against us. The swaying of the train pushed her against me too regularly for clarity of thought.

'Italian?'

'Italian is good.'

'I'll take you to a little place I love.'

She took my arm and we headed through the crowds. I think I commented on various things, I have no idea, words just came out of my mouth. She spoke back to me and I tried to concentrate on what she was saying but my mind swirled in and out, I was so intently aware of her being so close.

We entered a narrow restaurant. The girl who greeted us was delighted to see Amy. Did she really know everyone? I smiled as I was introduced, instantly forgetting her name. Then we sat down at a table and I took a deep breath.

'That was rather hectic.'

'I love the crowds,' she said. 'Especially when there's a carnival or New Year's ...'

'Or Camden on a weekend ...'

'That's true, the whole world descends on Camden.'

My nerves were starting to calm down. I just needed to hold out a little longer without saying or doing anything stupid and I would be all right.

'Where did you grow up?' Amy asked.

I blinked, paused. She was asking personal information and we'd only just sat down.

'New Zealand.'

'Really?'

'A town called Timaru.'

'What was it like?'

'Oh, great, I enjoyed it.'

'No, no,' laughed Amy. 'I need a description. What it looked like, the people, your school, that sort of thing.'

I smiled. I wasn't used to someone leaping into my personal life.

She leaned forward.

'I want to find out about you and as we're having dinner we've got ages to talk.'

For what purpose, I wanted to say. Do you like me, are we really on a date, or is this how you get to meet all your friends?

I tapped my foot gently on the floor. I often found that calmed my mind down, because if she was here on what she thought was a date then I wasn't sure I could hold a normal conversation. Random nonsensical words were going to come out of my mouth very soon.

I took a deep breath and told her about my school. And before long I was telling her about my family. And then university and my friends and what we had got up to, and she'd told me nothing at all about herself, but somehow it was all going smoothly.

'You're very lucky to have gone to university.'

'Didn't you?'

She laughed.

'What?'

'I left school as soon as I could.'

'Really?'

'Yes.'

'Really?'

'I hated school, having to sit at a desk for hours hearing boring information about things I wasn't interested in. Most of my school time I spent dreaming about living in a lighthouse.'

'And did you?'

'Of course! I spent the first two years on a lighthouse down in Cornwall.'

'Was it lonely?'

'No no, we weren't far from a village and they were lovely people. It gave me a chance to clear my head. And I read loads of books.'

'Must have been extraordinary.'

'It was, life is extraordinary.'

She smiled.

'I bet none of your friends dropped out of school.'

'A couple dropped out of university,' I laughed.

'I've never regretted it.'

'No, I'm not surprised.'

She was no ordinary girl, not in any sense.

'So why do you work at the pet shop?'

'I enjoy it. I love animals, I meet people who love animals, and the children adore visiting.'

'Doesn't it get a little dull?'

'Sometimes, but stopping and watching a goldfish swimming around gives me a good feeling. I never get bored. I don't mind doing nothing and I love silence as much as I love the loudness of the city.'

'You are quite amazing.'

She laughed, and I laughed. I hadn't meant to say that out loud, not the sort of thing you're supposed to say.

'Shall we order?'

We had dinner. A fantastically cheap meal with little flavour, but I didn't care, I knew I was in love. It was sort of like having a bucket of freezing cold water thrown in my face, shocking but exhilarating.

Afterwards we wandered down to the Embankment, Amy holding me close.

'Have you ever felt the soul of this city?' she asked.

'I don't think so.'

'Come with me.'

We walked quickly to Westminster Bridge and I followed her as she clambered down a narrow passageway and then up a small hidden ladder.

'This way. We're going to the middle of the bridge.'

There were two steel girders close together with meshing between them. Amy stood on the meshing and, spreading her arms out wide, she walked across the bottom of the bridge. Above was the roar of the traffic and below were the dark currents of the Thames.

I was sure this was not a good idea but she was already a dozen feet from me.

I climbed up gingerly, shaking a little, and spread my arms out slowly.

It was terrifying. The traffic was unbelievably loud, making the bridge shake, and underneath the river was dark and menacing.

The wind grew stronger as I got closer to the middle where Amy was waiting for me.

'Isn't it gorgeous?' she yelled.

I didn't reply, intent on getting one foot in front of another without tripping.

Finally I reached her.

'Up here,' she called.

She disappeared up a ladder into a hole above us. I

followed, there was nothing else to do.

We climbed to the top of the bridge above the traffic. Each time I planted a foot on a rung I was sure I was going to fall. I could hardly breath and tears ran down my face from the wind.

'We're here!'

A tiny platform.

'No one knows about this. I only found it by studying the plans.'

I stood, Amy helping me, now daring to look around.

There were the buildings, the lights, the traffic, the river, the boats, two planes in the sky. It was phenomenal.

'Now lift up your hands and breathe.'

I lifted my hands, raised my eyes, and breathed in the cold air. Then I felt it, a rush, like being caught in a river about to fall over a waterfall. It filled me, overwhelmed me, the world was inside me, its heart pounding, its lungs breathing, the city with a million emotions, whirling, racing, dancing like a maniac on the edge of the earth.

'Do you feel it?'

'Yes!' I shouted.

I laughed, and as I laughed, Amy kissed me. And the passion of the city pounded through us, the wonder, the beauty, the surging of the water, the stars above, within and without, flowing from the city through us and out again, the hopes and dreams of its inhabitants, the joy, the exhilaration of being alive.

I grabbed her tight and shared the wonder of the city. I opened myself to share all I was, all that I wanted to be, my desperation to love and be loved, my being passing into hers, and her passing into me, all the love she had for this world, all the tears she shed for others, all her dreams for the lives of those who lived in this city.

I closed my eyes and lost myself in her, completely, totally. I was no longer my own, I was hers, I was the city's. I gave my life away, it would never again be my own.

Chapter Twenty Four

We didn't sleep that night, just spent hours drinking coffee, talking, lying on our backs in St James's Park gazing at the stars, meeting all sorts of people who were wandering around, unable or not wanting to sleep.

Morning came and we walked along The Mall back to the city.

'Fancy breakfast?' I asked.

'Love to,' Amy replied.

A vendor had just opened his tiny corner sandwich shop. We chose some pastries and drinks.

'I love watching the city wake up,' said Amy, sitting down on a bench.

I gave her a kiss and sat back, enjoying the food and being beside Amy, as the number of cars and pedestrians gradually increased to a whirl of activity.

It was mesmerising. I could feel the city pulling people away from their homes and families, sucking them in like a giant magnet. And they were powerless to resist. They moved quickly, automatically, looking straight ahead.

Occasionally there were the drifters, those who were wandering, choosing different directions, not going anywhere in particular. They were fascinating to watch, to guess what their next move would be, what they were thinking, what they had done in their past that they now carried old rucksacks and fossicked in rubbish bins.

'I'm seeing a couple more artists today. Do you want to

come?'

'I've got to work.'

I'd completely forgotten.

'But I'll see you after work and I'll expect you to be early!' she said.

Then she kissed me and turned and ran down the cobblestones towards the tube station, not because she was late but because she enjoyed running.

I took a deep breath. It was going to be a great day.

Karla worked in Pimlico in a hidden away garage. I knocked loudly on the door. There wasn't any answer but I could hear loud music inside. I pushed the door open and was blinded by a welding torch.

I closed my eyes and slid into the side of the room.

The welding machine and radio were turned off.

'Hey!'

'Hey!'

'Charles?'

'Yes.'

'Sit yourself down on that seat and I'll be over in a minute.'

I hurried to the seat and looked around the rest of the room. It was a mess, twisted bits of metal and old glass bottles.

'Finished! Do you want to see our work?'

'Love to.'

'This way.'

And off she went, walking quickly out the door and back to the tube station.

'Two to Brixton.'

She purchased the tickets and strode down the escalators.

A train arrived and we got on. I wasn't sure if she wanted me to talk, so I sat there silently.

'We have to work at night when the trains have stopped.'

I nodded.

'Here's the first one.'

I didn't know what I was looking for and hoped I didn't miss it. Not that there was a chance of that. Graffiti is the word that initially sprung to mind, if graffiti wasn't created with spray paint but with glittering broken glass and bright lights fifty feet long with images of London and huge words describing the city. The reflected light filled the carriage with colour, all over the walls and floor. The passengers almost leapt out of their seats.

Karla smiled.

'We've put up ten so far along the line.'

'They're huge!'

'Some of them are on straight track, some of them go round corners. Those ones are more fun. They're like driving through an exploding star. There's one coming up after the next station.'

I sat very still, filled with anticipation. We careered through the tunnels, then suddenly the train filled with light. The glass was on both sides of the tunnel creating millions of different coloured splinters of colour. It was just as Karla had said, like travelling through an exploding star, the train on the tracks felt like it was out of control, no sense of up or down, gravity lost. Then the darkness of the tunnel returned and I was left with a pounding heart.

'A rush!'

'Yes,' I agreed, breathless. 'A rush, amazing.'

'Want to see some more? They're all different.'

'Love to.'

So we travelled on to Brixton, hurtling through stars, then we returned to Pimlico.

'Come and meet my team.'

I spent the next hour being introduced to a dozen teenagers who worked in two garages and an old church hall in Pimlico. They were intense, fiercely proud of their project.

I left the hall and took a deep breath. They had literally blown my mind with their art and their passion.

Chapter Twenty Five

Lunch with Tim was in order. I had a shower and a shave, then threw back on my clothes and strode through to his office.

'Tim!'

'Charles!'

'Lunch?'

'Now?'

'Now is good.'

'Great!'

He closed his book and we left.

'I expect you've got all sorts of stories to tell me.'

'Like you wouldn't believe.'

'You forget I read all day long, there's little in real life that is more surprising than fiction.'

'Depends if the writers have experienced real life.'

'The power of the imagination is greater than the experience of the senses.'

'Only for the reader who never dares to experience the world of the senses. Then the imagined starts to pale.'

'You do have some stories to tell.'

'A few, nothing like the stories I'll be able to tell in a year's time. I've only just started.'

'An urban adventure. Perhaps you should write a book of your own. About time you did something creative.'

'Perhaps I should.'

We sat under an umbrella, cool amidst the heat of the

burning sun.

'I'm coming back to work.'

'So soon?'

'I've got a cunning plan.'

Tim laughed.

'We're in trouble!'

'I've met a number of people who write, and I'm sure there's tons more out there, people who live on the streets, in the hostels …'

'Under bridges …'

'That's the idea. And I think we could publish their work.'

'You say that in the plural.'

'And there are artists who are producing phenomenal work.'

'And you want to publish books of their work as well?'

'Yes.'

Tim paused.

'Well, why not?' he pondered. 'You'll have to show me, of course, give me a taste of what we're getting ourselves into, but if you're convinced?'

'I am.'

'And we never say no to a good idea.'

'Never!'

'And you'll still keep your current job as well? I had a vague idea we could get by without you but I'm afraid you're indispensable.'

'That's a relief.'

We tucked into lunch. It was fantastic.

'So are you going to stay living rough?'

'No, I don't think so, bit uncomfortable.'

'Park benches bad for the back?'

'I feel pretty sore in the morning.'

'But you'd get used to it.'

'Maybe.'

'And your plan?'

'First up I've got to get some more books for the Chanel Girls, then I've got to see some more artists I'm writing articles about, and I tell stories to a group of children, I'm called *Charlie The Clown*. And of course I'm going to track down the poets for our first anthology.'

'And we'll see you in the office every so often?'

'Every so often. I've only started, Tim. Who knows what I'm going to find to fill in my days. I can't guarantee anything. Tomorrow something else will appear. I've only opened my eyes for a few days and it's been such a blast. Every new person I meet provides another opportunity. In six months my life may have changed completely.'

'Perhaps you could introduce me to some of these weird and wonderful people.'

'Really?'

'Of course. You're starting to make me jealous. I don't want to be missing out.'

'Then meet me at your old park bench tonight. Set your alarm for midnight.'

'To do what?'

'That's the fun bit, I have no idea.'

I went to the supermarket to buy supplies for my dinner with Jess and Andrew that night. A bit tricky given a park bench doesn't have any cooking facilities, so I decided to go for cold meat, bread, salad, fruit and cheeses, with champagne. It was, I had decided, my last night sleeping on the park bench and the end of being poor, so I used my credit card.

I was early to meet Amy, why wouldn't I be? I'd been itching to see her all day but had held off, trying not to look desperate. The anticipation as I walked along the street was almost unbearable. I forced myself not to run but I couldn't stop myself, I ran like a silly boy to the pet shop and came to a halt just before it, got my breath back, then peered round the door.

She wasn't there!

I was so filled with the excitement of seeing her, of holding and kissing her, that I was completely dumbfounded. She wasn't there, she'd gone, perhaps she'd gone back to Cornwall.

I turned away and there she was, crossing the road, smiling. She ran and threw her arms around me, kissing me.

Then she stood back, crossed her arms and looked very cross.

'Where have you been all day?'

'I saw some art on the tube, and ...'

'You didn't come and visit me!'

'No, ah ...'

'You should have dropped by, every hour, on the hour, and you didn't turn up once!'

'No, I ...'

'Charles!'

'I'm sorry, I didn't want to disturb you.'

'I work at a pet shop, I love being disturbed.'

'I ...'

I didn't really want to blurt out that I didn't want to appear desperate, that she was so wonderful and beautiful that I longed to hold her and stay with her every second of the day. That I hadn't talked about her to Tim because I would have had to leave and run to see her.

'Charles?'

I blurted out that I didn't want to appear desperate, that she was so wonderful and beautiful that I longed to hold her and stay with her every second of the day. And I had fought myself to stay away so I didn't appear ridiculous.

She frowned once more, then burst into a huge smile.

'Well, that's alright then! But don't do it again. I want to see you all the time for at least the next six months. That's what being in love is all about!'

She kissed me, dragged me into the shop and got me to help clean up, which was hard to do being in a daze and only wanting to stare at the beautiful girl who had just proclaimed our love.

'What's for dinner?'

I showed her the contents of the bag.

'Yum! Leave it here and we'll pick it up after we've spent an hour lying in the park together.'

She took my hand and off we went to lie in the afternoon sun, dreamily gazing at each other and the world passing us by.

Chapter Twenty Six

Dinner started off with the four of us, Jess, Andrew, Amy and myself. But it was never going to end that way, not where we were sitting by the canal and with the numbers of people the others knew. Soon word spread and there were a dozen, then a couple of dozen. An extraordinary mix of people, from the girls at the hostel and a few old guys that stank of whisky, to artists, business people and a couple from one of the houses along the canal. The police wandered along, hearing of a gathering, and they stopped for a while to have something to eat. Everyone had some food and drink to add, sharing it round, enjoying themselves.

It got darker and Jess got out four old fashioned lanterns that she hung from the trees above us. One of the old guys lined up candles along the edge of the canal and lit them.

'Now it's time for some entertainment,' said Jess loudly. 'Julian! Play something for us.'

A thin bearded man stepped forward.

'It would be an honour,' he said, bowing slightly.

He took his time unpacking his violin case and tuning the instrument.

'I shall play you something I wrote yesterday,' he declared. 'For all those who are in love.'

He raised his bow and began.

It was extraordinarily delicate, haunting, beautiful, the music mingling with the sound of the water, tripping lightly, delicately, making us smile. Across the way people peered out from behind the curtains of houses and then opened their windows and leaned out. A couple came down to the canal, hand in hand, caught up in the wonder of the music.

I kissed Amy. The music, the night sky, the canal, the candles, the presence of so many wonderful people. I felt like I had been living in the wilderness all my life.

The piece finished and Julian bowed, allowing himself a small smile in response to the rapturous applause.

'And now a little dancing?' he asked, a twinkle in his eye.

'Yes!' everyone agreed.

He nodded and raised his bow. Then he brought it down and began to play. Immediately two of the younger guys ran to get the drums they had left by the trees and joined in. A girl opened her case and brought out a flute.

We took each other's hands and began to dance. It was exhilarating, literally kicking up our heels, going from one person to the next, linking arms and twirling them round, laughing, whooping. Over on the other side of the canal people were also dancing, couples and families. Our group was growing larger, filling the pathway down to the bridge.

Julian played on and on until we were exhausted and collapsed on the ground.

There was silence for a minute while we caught our breath. Then Andrew stood up.

'And now some poetry. Lana!'

A tall dark haired woman stood in the middle of the group. She gazed about her with a soft smile.

'A new poem,' she said, in a deep, mellow voice. 'A poem of new life, of new love.'

She stood very tall, her back arching, and began.

'Sun splinters drops of pure water
about the risen mountains.
A bird flitters into life
as day dawns.
And the strength of beauty
brushes away early dewed mist.
Here then is love.
A seeking
into the wonders
of God's natural worlds.
Love,
leaping from shore to shore,
whistling the joy
of a new-born hope.
And changing,
forever changing,
under the earth-bounden light
of the heavens above.'

She nodded her head and raised her hands towards the darkened sky.

'Love catching, tripping, hopping onto the wind.
Wings of hope,
swishing through deserted grasslands,
floating through sprinkled clouds,
hushing the waves.
There to rest.
There to wait.
Until the crag of a mountain peak catches hold
and the hope of inner surprise
is hoisted to the heights of joy.'

Lana lowered her arms and bowed. We smiled in agreement, there was no need for applause, it would have ruined the beauty of the moment.

'Is this what you are searching for?' whispered Amy.

I paused and looked around me. Both sides of the canal were filled with people, silent, surrounded by lanterns and candles. Jess was whispering to Julian and a girl who was with him. She was short and thin and looked as though she hadn't eaten for a week. Her hair was tangled, her clothes were dirty and the bones in her face stood out in the candle light. She couldn't have been more than sixteen. A boy sat beside her, listening, nodding. He looked just as young, just as hungry.

The three of them stood silently. The crowd hushed, expectant.

Then Julian began playing, and the boy and the girl danced, ballet, a duet, it was the most beautiful art I had ever seen, creating images with their bodies, separating and coming together again, falling in love, hesitating, then daring. Finally kissing.

The crowd was mesmerised, no one could move, the world beyond the two dancers no longer existed. Then they smiled, embarrassed, humble, and we clapped, clapped so hard it hurt. And they waved to us, then sat down, avoiding the acclaim.

I turned to Amy. I was surrounded by the people of Camden, from all walks of life, and I was overwhelmed and inspired by their art and their lives. I was passionately in love and had discovered something to which I could fully could commit my life.

'Yes,' I whispered. 'This is what I was searching for.'

She smiled.

'And it's always been here. You've just learnt how to open your eyes.'

'A little wider.'

'Yes, a little wider.'

Jess stood up again.

'I think we should dance some more, don't you?'

We all agreed, leaping to our feet, and we danced again, from one to another, sharing smiles and laughter, our eyes filled with the wonder of the night and the beauty around us, danced till we couldn't breath anymore we were so exhausted.

The crowd gradually dissipated, people wandering away until there was just the four of us left sitting on the bench. I glanced at my watch.

'Tim should be here soon.'

'Why?'

'I wanted him to meet Liam Norwood.'

'Is that Tim?' asked Amy.

A tall man was walking quickly towards us.

'Tim!'

'Charles!'

'You made it.'

'Didn't get mugged.'

'No, although you're good at that.'

He smiled.

'Introduce me then.'

I'd just finished going round our little group when we heard more footsteps.

Amy ran to the old poet and threw her arms around him.

'It's been too long, Liam. You should visit me more often.'

'I'm sorry my little angel but a poet has no sense of time.'

He took her arm and they joined our group. He knew everyone except Tim.

'And are you a night person such as myself, Tim?' Liam asked.

'I work during the day and enjoy the night.'

'Then you must tell me about your work. Shall we walk and talk?'

He assumed agreement and started up the path. We let them go, following a little way behind.

At the second bridge they stopped and waited for us to catch up. As we continued, I asked Liam if he'd ever published his poems.

'I have no need.'

'I understand. But I would like to publish your poems, to have others read them. And to publish the poetry of your fellow poets.'

'My fellow poets?'

'Yes.'

'How do you know there are other poets?'

'I am assuming.'

He stopped.

'You assume correctly. Would you like to meet them?'

I nodded.

'They may be interested in your desire to publish their work. But I must warn you, they are not used to being told what to do. They will only do whatever they choose.'

We walked with the old man up the steps and along to the

park that was lit by the moon.

'Here are my friends. I wish that you treat them with respect.'

He bent under the branch of a tree and there they were, gathered in a circle, silent.

'Greetings,' said Liam. 'I have brought some friends.'

We were introduced and space was made for us. Then, one by one, they recited their poetry. No one had written anything down, there were no introductions, no explanations. Just six old, gray, bearded men, reciting poetry that was filled with hope and joy and wisdom in their deep and languid tones, surrounded by the aged trees that were silent and listening.

We sat there for hours in a trance-like state, our minds being awakened to the dreams of the ancients. Finally they finished and they rose, without speaking, and disappeared into the stillness of the night.

On the way back, Tim and I lingered behind the others. The water flowed, the trees whispered to each other, the full moon hung in the sky. Before me walked three figures near a canal, walking slowly, peacefully, completely at one with the world about them.

Chapter Twenty Seven

June 2005, a very hot day in London. I decided to take a break from work and wander up to Regents Park where I lay down under the shade of a tree.

I took off my shoes and socks and glanced around. There were a few regulars, lots of tourists, some people crazily jogging in the heat. Others lay spread-eagled, naked but for their underwear.

A girl cycled towards me on an old fashioned bike. She had long dark hair, possibly Spanish, and wore her clothes like she enjoyed them, no fuss, just threw them on. She slowed as she got nearer and smiled, the most beautiful of smiles.

'This is for you.'

In her hand was a four leafed clover. I let it fall into my open palm, we kissed, then she pushed down on her pedal and was off.

I had a tingling down my spine. A beautiful girl doesn't give you a four leafed clover every day. Only once every few years!

Back at the office things were laid back and peaceful. Not like three years ago. We had literally been overrun by success. It had all started with the publication of a small book of poetry by the old friends of Liam Norwood. What should have been an unnoticeable moment in publishing history was changed when Edward Hays from *The Guardian* decided it was noteworthy. From his article it grew to the other broadsheets, then *The Sun* decided that several million readers would be interested in these old men and their poetry, then on to television. The media couldn't get enough of what these men had to say, they adored them. They were treated with respect, their poems were taken seriously, they were celebrities.

We couldn't keep pace with demand for the book, and then we introduced the world to not only more poetry, but also the art books which included the stories of the artists written in their own words, literally, they were handwritten notes alongside the images.

Tim and I and the rest of the office enjoyed the success for six months, but one morning we discovered neither of us had time to have lunch.

'Lunch?'

'When?'

'I don't know.'

'I'm too busy.'

'So am I.'

'So busy we can't have lunch?'

'That doesn't sound right.'

'No it doesn't.'

'Something is wrong, Tim.'

'Very wrong.'

'We should be able to have lunch.'

'So we will have lunch.'

'They'll have to wait.'

'Absolutely.'

We both paused, knowing we had back to back meetings scheduled during the day.

'Shall we?'

'We shall.'

We walked out the door. As we went people called after us, reminding us about meetings that were about to happen.

'To the pub?'

I nodded, and we purposefully strode away from the office, down the steps to the canal.

We ordered and sat back.

'I was thinking about hiring more staff,' said Tim.

'We are a tad busy,' I ventured.

We both paused, then burst into laughter. It was such a relief to laugh, it broke through the stressful bubble that surrounded our conversations at work.

'How did this happen? We're supposed to be enjoying ourselves.'

'All my fault.'

'Definitely! You are to blame. How dare you make us so successful!'

The beers arrived.

'Here's to someone else doing the work,' Tim raised his glass.

I raised mine in agreement.

'And here's to those crazy old men!'

We hired ten extra staff within a fortnight and opened an operations office down the road. A functional space with computers and workstations which allowed Tim to retreat to his couch and beloved literature.

As for me, I set up a number of poetry readings in the local hostels. All sorts came, everyone was welcome. I organised them in large meeting rooms with loads of food and great coffee. Anyone could read anything. We laughed, we cried, we were inspired, sometimes we were offended. But we were all friends, we got to know each other and spent time after the poetry eating and sharing stories.

It was at a hostel in Kings Cross where, just after we had sat down and begun, a man walked in. He was tall, thin, his clothes were hanging off him. He hesitantly took a seat at the back and immediately bowed his head low avoiding the others.

When we had been round the group and it seemed that everyone had read their poems, he finally looked up. His eyes were overly large in their hollow sockets and his cheekbones stuck out without a decent covering of flesh.

'I have a poem,' he said, his voice quiet and faltering.

I nodded and he reached into his pocket and drew out a scrumpled piece of paper.

'It doesn't have a title.'

People smiled and murmured encouragement.

Then he took a breath and went to begin, and at that moment I realised who he was, the man who had killed Antya.

'I didn't know her
I had never seen her before.
She was standing there
Handing out food
Sharing
Caring
Beautiful, loving,
And I was a monster,

Full of hatred,
And I hated her,
I don't know why.
I held the knife,
So sharp,
And when she hugged me,
I hated her more,
So I turned the knife inside her.
Now I cannot sleep,
I cannot eat.
I hate myself for my hate.'

There was complete silence in the room. The man stood there, his hands shaking, and the paper dropped to the floor. Tears filled his eyes as he shrugged.

I walked to him, the image of Antya so clear before me. He kept his head raised, prepared for the blow, recognising that I knew who he was.

I stood before him and paused. I was shaking. I wanted to destroy this monster, this man who had mercilessly killed a girl who lived to help others.

But as I stared into his eyes, my whole being enraged against him, I saw that he too was starting out on a journey just as I had, one I could never hope to understand, one of pain and anguish. That coming to this place and reading this poem was the hardest thing for him, that he was not redeemed, he wasn't asking for forgiveness, but he was admitting the evil within him to this small group of outcasts. And to himself. And to say this out loud was the beginning of his journey.

I finally discovered within myself what I had seen in Antya's eyes that day as she lay on the street dying. That there is hope within everyone, even the man who had killed her.

I hugged this man who hated himself.

We stood there for an age. Then I broke away and extended my hand.

'Charles.'

He stood up straight.

'James,' he said, his hand taking mine.

'James, you're very welcome. I'd like to introduce you to my friends.'